T0157111

It's Not Over Yet,
A Love Story

Tona Gardner

authorHOUSE®

AuthorHouse™
1663 Liberty Drive
Bloomington, IN 47403
www.authorhouse.com
Phone: 1-800-839-8640

Published by AuthorHouse   06/27/2012

ISBN: 978-1-4772-3216-3 (sc)
ISBN: 978-1-4772-3215-6 (e)

Library of Congress Control Number: 2012911616

Many Thanks To

My Children for giving me a purpose in life

Elaine which without her this would have never been finished

All the friends that helped me make it to the end

Prologue

What will make you want to read my story? Love or happiness, maybe it is danger and cruelty. Some may want to read those hot sexy love senses, could that be you? Might it be to find a better way of life; or to see the pain and heartaches that life has to offer?

This story has it all. It will have you on the edge of your seat. At times it will allow you to sit back and relax.

This has been the hardest story I have written. It could be the hardest you ever read; and some will be unable to read it at all. Those are the ones that must read it.

To be a witness to the worse that humans have to offer, and is off set by the best and kindness there is.

Come along; take the walk through life with one small child. See and feel what made her into the lady she became. She only wanted what we all want; love and happiness. But, her road may be harder for even her to walk. Come along, be there to yell when need be or hug her when she can hardly move.

Right to the last page she will need help, the story will never be over. Her life as well as yours will never die even

Tona Gardner

when death comes. This story will live on and will amaze even those that read it after she is gone.

For you that can make it to the end, it can become a guide for those that follow. Maybe you can be the one to make the difference.

Contents

The Beginning

Come with me to my little corner of the world.

It is safe for me here, in my little corner.

Can you see my little corner of the world?

Let me take you there, I will show you its wonders.

Look this is pain, poof it is gone just like that.

Anger comes and goes leaving no marks to be seen.

Hurt, knocks on the door, but it cannot enter here.

Look, can you see the blue skies, hear the birds sing?

My little corner has a name, it is called fantasy;

I am called lost childhood.

9-3-1966

Chapter One

L iving in a world of make-believe was second nature to me. A childhood of abuse, disappointments, and fear had made it necessary. I had created a family that any child would love to call their own.

When my father was at home alone with me and my baby brother, things would happen. At such a young age I didn't have words, I didn't understand what was happening. At the age of three I knew what made me happy; candy, toys, and splashing in the bath tub water. There was pain and fear which happened when I was bad. I must have been bad, I don't know why, but that is what my little brain was telling me.

Before long I would learn how to remove myself from the abuse. I went into my 'happy world' where daddy gave me candy and helped me build a tower with my blocks. It was not me there in the bedroom; it was some other little girl. I couldn't linger on that thought; I had to stay with the good daddy.

As I got older, I started saying things that would make my father mad. The time he spent with me became less and less. Then my mother was pregnant again and she stopped working. She was home all the time now. It was over. Not only in my life but in my brain which started to believe it never happened; all that was left was my fear of him, the only outward sign that showed, mother could never understand it.

Mom stayed at home even after my baby sister was born and Dad had to also get a day job. As time passed my fear of him moved to the very back of my brain and in my dreams.

As all little girls do, I began to grow and develop. It wasn't just me that noticed, but my older brother took notice of me. Generally my brother would have nothing to do with me; I was just his dumb little sister.

One night when mom and dad were out, he changed his mind as to who I was. All we kids were tucked in bed and fast asleep. I felt someone get into my bed, it was my older brother.

"Get out of my bed or I will tell the babysitter." For some reason I felt a deep fear of him.

"Quiet." He put his hand over my mouth. "Listen, sis, I am worried because you are getting older," he moved his hand from my mouth and patted my head, "I want to teach you some things, so you can be like other girls. If you want to be liked and have boyfriends, you have to know these things." He moved his hand from the top of my head to my breast, "they are small but they will get bigger."

"Stop that! It hurts." I tried to move his hand away. "Ouch, that hurts, stop it."

"See that is what I mean." He moved his hand to my other breast and squeezed it too. "All the girls that have boyfriends do this and it will feel good after you get used to it."

"It hurts too much." Getting the words out was becoming harder and harder; fear was covering every thought in my mind. My brother could be cruel at times.

"Here I will just rub them a little more, soon it won't hurt anymore; it will feel good to you." He now had one hand on each breast and rubbing them and squeezing them; "You don't want boys to think you are dumb and ugly. You will never have a boyfriend."

I just laid there out of so much deep fear; then I could feel my mind slip away. I could almost see beautiful blue skies, almost hear birds singing, and then he was gone. I was alone in bed, did that happened or was I dreaming? Then I realized my pj top was wide open.

My brother kept out of my sight for the next few days. Then again he joined me in the middle of the night. Everyone was asleep and quiet, except the faint snoring coming from behind mom's closed bedroom door. It started much like the first night, but just as I started to see blue skies I was pulled back to where I really was. "What are you doing?' I pushed his head away from my breast.

"Don't be afraid, you have to know about this. Guys will want to do this."

"Why!" I asked.

"It makes them like you more," he said. "You know Mike?"

I nodded my head trying not to shake too much.

"Well, I know he kind of likes you. But, he won't for long if you don't know how to do the things all his girlfriends do this with him. All girlfriends do this." He again moved his head to my breast. Opening his mouth, he began moving from one small breast to the other. The shakes had stopped, I just lay there my body was limp, my mind was elsewhere.

The next morning my breasts were real sore and red. As we left the house for school my brother pulled me aside. "Don't say anything to Mike, just act like you don't know anything. He will think you are chasing him. Give it time; you are not ready for him yet. He won't like you very long right now. Just don't say or do anything to anybody or else!" I knew what 'or else' meant.

Fear kept me from saying anything to Mom She would just get mad at me and call me dumb. I also wanted Mike to like me, I had a need to have someone like me.

A few days later, we kids were out in the backyard, some of the neighborhood kids came to join us. We had this old 45 record player out there; we were playing records and dancing with each other. Well, they were dancing with each other, I was dancing alone. My brother came over to me, pulled me further out back behind the garage.

"Sis, ask Sueie to spend the night on Friday." He put his hand on my shoulder and squeezed real hard.

Moving out of his reach, I asked, "Why? She doesn't like me; she won't even say 'Hi' to me." Sueie was a bit older than me, already twelve. She was a popular girl, long blond hair and much more developed than myself. Inside I always wished I looked just like her.

"She told me she would be your friend if you asked her to spend the night." He was speaking very low and right in my face.

"I'll try;" I turned and walked away. I was always afraid to be so close to him,

Friday came and so did Sueie. Out back playing records Sueie did talk to me, even showed me a new dance step. She told me to keep practicing it. She spent most of the night with my brother, dancing, laughing, and touching each other everywhere.

When it came time to go to bed, we put on our pajamas. Mine was a two piece top and full bottoms. Sueie's was an all pink baby doll that you could see through. We lay in my double bed talking just like two old friends. Actually she asked questions about my brother and I answered. Sometime in the middle of the night I woke up and Sueie was gone. I thought she was in the bathroom I rolled over and went back to sleep. Even later, you could just see the light of day coming through the window, I awoke to movement, Sueie was crawling into bed, her hair was all a mass and a smile on her face, "Go back to sleep it is too early to get up yet," she said and rolled over and went fast to sleep. I did the same.

For the next several weeks Sueie did talk to me a lot and even invited me over to swim in her pool; of course my brother was always there. Sueie would spend one night a week and she would always disappear. It all stopped when Sueie and my brother had a big fight. She stopped talking to me and spending the night. It was all over as quick as it started. The ending of one thing, is the beginning of another.

My brother started visiting me again in the middle of the night. He started talking about Mike again. I was so happy about having friends I had forgotten all about Mike. There it was back on my mind, but, I still didn't like doing these things. When I told him, he laughed. "Sueie really liked all these things and more. You saw how happy she was in the mornings." He got this big smile and a look on his face I had never seen before. "She also taught me a few new things to do that I know will really make Mike like you; maybe even love you." He moved his hand from my breast to the top of my pajama bottoms. "You have to do same things to me as I am doing them to you, you have to, otherwise it won't work." He moved his hand inside both my pajamas and underpants. "Now you do the same." With his free hand he took my hand and pushed it into his underpants to his penis, "Put your hand around this and rub it up and down." He froze. "Not so hard, slow and easy." He moved his hand to my private part and started to rub it. I wanted to see my blue skies so bad, but each time I slowed down he would pinch my private part, it would hurt. It would keep me there in my bed with him. "Don't stop!" he would say. When he left, there was so much fear in me, my mind and right to my bones. I just lay there shaking.

So it went until the end of school that year. He would visit my bed, teaching me; tell me by summer I would be the kind of girl Mike would love. There were also girls that would become my best friend, talking to me and spending the night. I really didn't like these girls but I did like it when my brother left me alone. Shortly after summer break started and between his girlfriends, my brother came again to my bed.

"Mike asked me if you would make a good girlfriend;" he said while opening my pajama top.

Mike, did he say Mike wanted me as a girlfriend? "What did you tell him?"

"I told him you might, you were a little young. He would have to come over some day and find out for himself." Moving his hand down, "Remember what I told you." Taking my hand and moving it where he wanted it. "You will have to remember this so Mike will like you and think you are grown up." Getting that strange look on his face when my hand touched him; "You will have to do more than this with Mike to really be his girlfriend."

"What else is there I have to do?" I pulled my hand back that deep fear was setting in again.

"I'll teach you. Take off your panties" he started tugging at my pajama bottoms. "This is the best part, you will really like it and so will Mike." He spread my legs and got on top of me.

Pain, a pain I don't remember ever feeling before. "Stop; stop it hurts!"

He moved is hand over my mouth. "Don't wake up mom or dad; they will be really mad at you." He never moved his hand from my mouth until he got up to leave.

It hurt so bad; I could never do this again. I thought this is wrong; people wouldn't do this, it hurts too much. I stayed in my room for two days. I told mom I was feeling sick, which I really was. On the third day I came out to watch a bit of television.

"Feeling better now?" My brother asked.

"Yes, better." I couldn't even look at him. That night he came again.

"Sorry I hurt you, I went too fast, tonight I will go slowly."

Yes, there was pain again, but I didn't say so, and it wasn't as bad. The next day, my brother told me Mike will be coming over Monday, that he had told him that I was acting more mature. Mom and Dad would be at work. And there were no babysitters. My parents thought my brother was old enough to watch us. If he had any trouble, Judy, the lady next door would help.

He came again that night. "One more time, this time there will no pain, and you can really enjoy being with Mike."

He lied again, I wanted to cry, but I haven't cried for years.

On Monday Mike did come over, he did ask me if I would be his girlfriend, then he took me to my bedroom. I was both very happy and very afraid. I pretty much just laid there and did what I was taught. When he got up, I asked if he was going to kiss me and tell me that he loved me "I love you," then he kissed my cheek. He didn't stay much longer said he had to get home.

Mike never talked to me again. My brother said I wasn't good enough to be his girlfriend, but he would keep helping me until I was. So, through the next school year, things went on the same. I would have new girlfriends; my brother would come to my bed when he was between the girls. New boyfriends would come to me who my brother told me I had to like. When I tried to put a stop to it all, my brother would hurt me, not always bad, but bad enough. I became more and more withdrawn, spending as much time as I could with my blue skies, singing birds, and my happy family.

Near the end of school that year I overheard some girls talking. They were saying how this brother and sister wanted to be together and get married. One girl said it was a sin and they were going to burn in hell. I ran all the way home after school that day. Mom hadn't gotten home from work yet, so I went next door and talked to Judy. She had been a friend for years. I told her what I had heard at school. "Burn in hell," I asked if it was true? She agreed with the girls, saying brothers and sisters, fathers and daughters, or mothers and sons should never be together like that; it was just plain wrong and a big sin. Then she asked me if I wanted something to eat, so I guessed that was the end of our talk. "No thank you," I went home. I shut myself in my room. If I was ever going to cry it would be now, but no tears came. I was going to burn in hell, I was a bad person and I even felt like God was going to strike me dead. At this time in my life what had happened between my father and I was still blocked from my mind, all I knew was that my father really scared me. I would have to tell my brother it had to stop. I also knew I was very scared of him, since he could be very mean and hurtful when things happened that he didn't like, not that he was beating me up all the time, just now and then. He only pulled a knife on me once and the cut wasn't deep, but I guess I felt he could kill me if I talked about what was going on. I don't think I could tell him. That was when it hit me; I knew what I would have to do. I spent the rest of the day getting ready.

DearMom and Dad

I am leaving home. I can no longer live here with you. I am a very bad person. My brother and I have done bad things. I know you will never be able to love me again. God is going to kill me. Don't look for me; you will never see me again.

Good bye
Patty

I had everything packed and ready to go. My parents were going out so when everybody is in bed or asleep I would leave through the window. I had taken the screen off and checked to make sure I could open it. My plan was to go to the church near my school for the night. The next day I would go to school, nobody will know I ran away, nobody would think about looking for me there, who would run away to school? Then after school I would hit the road until dark. Then I would hide again until it was light again. I wish I wasn't so scared of the dark; I would have to find a place that was safe and had a light, like the church.

When it was all quiet and my brother was asleep in front of the T.V. out the window I went. It seemed the walk to the church took forever but, I finally made it. I was checking out everything in my bag to make sure I was ready for tomorrow. "No; No; No!" I forgot my homework. How could I go to school without it? What was I going to do, I was planning to leave after school, they would stop looking by then and I would be free to move. I had to go to school. I would just have to go back, sneak into my room and get my book with my homework. Leaving my bag at the church I headed for home.

When I reached my house, I saw that my bedroom light was on and Mom's car was in the drive way. My plans were going to have to change. I would get my bag and head for the hill tonight. I had always been afraid of that area because people would get lost and never be seen again. Well wasn't that what I needed?

Before I left, I just had to see what was going on. Very slowly and quietly I went to my bedroom window. It was still partly open the way I left it. Mom was sitting on my bed crying and holding my little sister. My father and brother were there too. My brother was saying he didn't know what I was talking about, he hadn't done anything wrong, "She is crazy always has been, she just wants to get me in trouble." Mom just kept crying, my sister was patting her head, she said she was sorry she didn't wake up but she hadn't heard anything. Which was true, she slept like the dead, nothing ever woke her up.

I left as slowly and quietly as I came. Heading back to the church to get my bag, I became worried that the police were out looking for me. Every time I saw a car coming I would hide behind something or just lay as flat as I could on the ground. It made slow going, it was giving me too much time to think. I kept thinking about Mom sitting there crying, I was starting to feel bad about hurting her. The thoughts of my crime were being replaced with my mom crying. Half way to the church I turned around and headed for home again. I kept hiding from any car; I wanted to go home not be put in jail. Slowly I made my way home. Through the window I could see my mom was still crying, I ran through the front door which was wide open; right to my bedroom and into my mom's arms. "I am sorry." I said over and over holding her as tight as I could. Finally her crying stopped.

"I love you, never ever do this again. It would kill me if something ever happened to you." She was holding me out in front of her. Tears were still running from her eyes.

"I'm sorry, I didn't want to hurt you; I'm sorry for what I did, I know I was wrong, I am so sorry." I was still shaking from fear and sorrow. She pulled me to her and told me everything would be alright. We will talk tomorrow.

"Go clean up and get into bed, I will be back to tuck you in." She kissed my forehead.

Then I remembered my bag at the church. Dad said he would take care of it. Sure enough he headed out with my brother. "Here it is" taking one step into my room and dropping my bag on the floor. "I hope there is no more talk about what you THINK you did that was so bad. You always have a way of making things seem worse than they are." His voice became very low and his eyes had that stare in them. "It's all in that dumb imagination of yours." He turned and left closing the door behind him.

Chapter Two

The next morning, after my younger brother and sister left for school, we all sat down in the living room. Mom wanted to know why I thought I had to run away. I looked at her, thinking she should know, why was she asking me. I looked at my father he was staring at me like he had the night before. I looked at my brother, he too was staring at me like he could kill me; maybe he could. His hands were all balled up into a fist and turning red.

Very quietly I began to talk, the words coming out very slowly; I needed to say the right thing. "I . . was . . scared . . I . . . I . . let . . him . . sleep . . with . . me." The words were very hard at coming, "I won't do it again, ever, I promise. Please don't hate me." I pleaded.

Mom looked at me, tears coming down, looking so sad, "I would never hate you, I will always love you." Reaching out her hands towards me, I didn't move or reach out. I believed her but, was afraid someday she could take it all back.

"I think it is time you two should know something we have never talked about." She looked from us to her husband. "Your father and I got married after both of you were born." She could plainly tell from the looks on our faces we were not understand just what she was saying. "Father was married before. He and his first wife had a baby and that was you," pointing to my brother. "I am not your real mother; I'm your step-mother. I love you as if you were my real son just like I do your brother and sister." Again she turned to her husband.

He turned his head towards us, "Son your real mother was a sick woman, and she was unable to be a mother to you or anyone. I had to take you away from her. You are very special to me." He turned his eyes on me "Patty your mother was also married before me and she had you. Sad as it sounds your real father didn't want your mother or you." The look in his eyes changed from hate to maybe love as he continued on. "The first time I saw you," pointing right at me, "You were just over one year old. I fell in love with you. You were the perfect little girl and I wanted to be your Daddy so bad. So your mother and I got married and became a happy family; we have been happy, right?" He sat back in his chair and his eyes dared me to disagree with him.

Mom was saying something about how this wouldn't change anything. My brother looked at me and smiled. Mom continued saying we could still be a happy family. I was hearing very little of what she was saying, my mind was reeling around and around. What does she mean, this doesn't change anything, it changes everything. "He is not my father; he is just your husband? He is not my brother; he is just your son;" pointing at the man that is not my father.

"This is true, he is your step-father and he is your step-brother," pointing at each as she spoke. "But they are still your family." Mom looked worried.

"So what do I call them?" I know she had no idea where I was heading.

"Just what you always have, Dad and brother," she was starting to feel a challenge from me.

"Why can I not just call him, Mr. or Bob," pointing at my step-father. "I could call him, BJ?" Swinging my finger around to land on my step-brother.

"I think this is enough, he is your father. You need to call him father. You can call your brother what you always have, Bobby," she said staring right into my eyes.

"I will think about it. But what about my other brother and sister; what are they to me?" I felt I needed to change the subject.

"Well, they are you half brother and sister and you will call them by the name you have always called them."

Maybe I won't burn in hell, I sure hope not. So this could be better news than I thought. I couldn't help the smile that came across my face.

Mom said that was that and things will go on as usual, and got out of her chair. She told us we would be cleaning today since we didn't go to school. So we all got up to do whatever we had to do. I was heading to my room when Mom stopped me, "I don't know what you were trying to do out there but I will not have any trouble. You will not hurt your Father or brother. Do you understand me?"

I told her yes and walked away. Is that all she cared about, their feelings, what about mine. Why didn't she say more about what my step-brother and I did, was it unimportant to her, did she think I was making it all up. Did she really love me? Maybe she did, but after her step-son, after my younger brother and sister and after my step-, no after Bob.

My whole life just changed and it is no little change, and nobody can see it. What is going to happen next?

Chapter Three

I graduated from the sixth grade and I was heading for Junior High school. I was happy about going to a new school; maybe I could make some friends, real friends.

At home I withdrew further and further away from the family. After all they weren't really my family. I had no family. It was a good thing for me that I meet Aunt Billie and Uncle Roady.

I spent more and more time at Aunt Billie's. She and her husband were good friends of my Mom and my step-father. They never had any children, even though they said they always wanted some. Aunt Billie was always very happy to have me over to spend time with her, as was Uncle Roady. Aunt Billie was nothing like my mother. Where my mom had dark hair and olive skin, Aunt Billie was blond with pale skin. Mom was slim and beautiful. Aunt Billie was a bit on the heavy side and more motherly looking. Aunt Billie had all the time in the world to spend with me, doing things I wanted to do. Mom was always too busy getting home from work after five and fixing dinner didn't leave any time with any of us kids, except on family nights. On those nights the family would play board games and eat all the popcorn we wanted.

On family nights everybody was to have their homework done by five. We didn't have any chores that night either. I was finding it harder and harder to get my homework done on time. I think I was spending more time day dreaming than working, maybe I planned it that way. If I didn't have homework I would say I didn't feel good and thought I should go right to bed. I just didn't want to partake in family night.

Almost all the other time I had free I was at Aunt Billie's house. They also had a big pool in their backyard, which was great because I loved to swim. Everybody called me a fish out of water. One day Uncle Roady asked if I would like a job taking care of the pool for them, he would pay me. I really didn't care about being paid; it meant that I could spend more time there.

"Yes, oh yes I would like that." Then I was almost afraid to say it but had to. "I don't know how to take care of a pool." Uncle Roady laughed a warm kind of laugh, the kind that is not at you but with you. He said he would show me how and even make a check list so I don't forget anything. He extended his hand to shake on it and I put my hand into his and we shook. "Deal" we both said.

Uncle Roady was a great teacher and very patient with me. Most the time when I did something wrong he would stand there arms crossed and a big smile on his face, a happy smile. He would stay that way until I got it right. I always knew when something was wrong. Then when I got it right he would laugh that laugh of his then say, "Good, what's next?" It didn't matter how many tries it took. I wanted him to be proud of me so I worked extra hard to remember how to do everything just right. In two weeks I was taking care of the pool all by myself. Uncle Roady would bring out the check list. I always got a check on each job. His eyes would twinkle as he smiled at me. "Another good job," he would say.

I was so happy that I was spending less time at home. Going straight to Aunt Billie's after school, she always helped me with my homework. On days I didn't have pool duty she would bring out her giant craft box, which had everything in it. Even daydreaming was happening more infrequently. It seemed only on family nights my homework wasn't finished on time. No one cared to ask why since they all thought I was too dumb to finish on time. I had very little conversation with anyone in the family and really didn't even know what was going on with any of them. So when the day came that a family meeting was called it was a shock to me.

We all gathered around the table, staring at each other. None of us kids had an inkling as to what was happening. Step-father stood up and announced, "The time has come, and your mother and I have been working very hard for this day. We are going to move into a new house. It will be bigger and better; each of you kids will have your own room. There will also be more than one bathroom, what more could we want?" He looked so proud of himself.

The chatter started right away, it seemed that everyone was happy about this. That is everyone except me. I didn't want to move, what if I couldn't see Aunt Billie or take care if the pool with Uncle Roady? No; I didn't like it at all. I stood up, (one of my moment of saying the wrong thing) so fast that my chair fell backwards, "Where will we be moving, I don't want to move from here," I demanded.

"We aren't sure just yet; we have just started to look." Mom could see the worry on my face. "We are looking in this same area for the right home. We would like you kids to be able to stay in the same schools."

Little did she know that that was not my worry? I didn't want to have to stay at home with this so called family; I wanted to spend time with Aunt Billie and Uncle Roady. I couldn't move from them, they were like my real mom and dad. The school or friends didn't matter. Maybe they were doing this because of me; they didn't want to see me happy. Maybe they thought if I got close enough to someone I would tell things they didn't want told.

It didn't matter how much I protested or refused to move. We moved into a big house across town, which might as well been in China. Mom told me that twice a week I could take the old school bus to Aunt Billie's to take care of the pool. She said she would pick me up on her way home from work. Somehow, my brain was saying, things have a way of not lasting long.

Taking the bus to Aunt Billie's lasted one month. "It is just too far for me to drive after work. I'm always late with dinner and that makes your father mad." She told me as a reason.

"I don't care if he gets mad or not. He isn't my father, he never cared about me, and he hates me." I yelled back at her.

"You are just a spoiled little brat. I said you can no longer take care of the pool. I will no longer pick you up. That is that last world." She turned to walk away, but stopped. "Why it is the only time you ever talk to us is when you want something, you act like you are not a part of this family."

"I am not; why doesn't anybody in this so called family ever cared about me, or how I feel. I have nothing to say to any of you that is why I don't talk."

After that I was never allowed to see or talk to Aunt Billie or Uncle Roady. Like I said good things never last.

Chapter Four

Our new big great house was not to make a family out of us. It didn't matter where we were living, things were wrong with this family. I wonder if I would have been better off not having that time with Aunt Billie or Uncle Roady, then I would have never know how caring, loving people could and should be. I wouldn't have missed it so much.

At home some strange things were happening. It seemed Mom and my step-dad was always mad at each other and with us kids. For me being sent to my bedroom was a good thing, having to do it night after night was even better, that is where I wanted to be.

One day I had to stay home from school because I was sick. Everybody left while I stayed in bed. A few hours passed and I was awakened by someone coming into the house. It was my step-father. The moment I saw him fear shot through me. "What are you doing here?"

"I just came home to check on you and to show the house to a friend." He moved aside and I saw a lady standing behind him. She looked like she was only a few years older than my step-brother.

"Nancy, this is my daughter, Patty. She wasn't feeling well today so she stayed home." He told her.

"He is my step-father, shouldn't you be in school yourself." I was a bit afraid to mouth off, but surly he wouldn't do anything in front of a stranger.

"You need to go to your bedroom and stay there!" He looked at me just like he could kill me.

I didn't say anything else went straight to my room. I really get enjoyment out of making him mad. This time he couldn't say much about it to anyone. They left about two hours later. I wondered how many times he came home when everybody was gone. He called me later to say if I ever wanted to go anywhere I was not to say anything about him coming home to anybody. I now know it wasn't the first time for a home visit.

Within six months Mom and step-dad were in divorce court. Step-dad moved in with is little friend, Nancy. She had two very small children so there wasn't much room. My step-brother would have to stay with us. So now there is another change in my life, and I was wrong to think it would get better.

Mom kept her day job and then started working three nights a week at a bar. She said step-father couldn't send enough money for her to make ends meet. Her working at a bar was like putting a candy junkie in a candy store. She was drinking three times more than when she was married.

Three weeks after mom stared working nights my past came to haunt me. I guess I got too relaxed, forgot good things don't last forever. While taking a shower, someone came into the bathroom; I couldn't see who it was. "Get out I'm in the shower;" I yelled.

"You didn't lock the door, how was I to know?" My step-brother said.

"Get out!" I yelled at him, with fear running all over me, I couldn't move.

"Don't worry; I'll lock it for you, chill." He stepped over to the door and locked it. But, he was on the inside.

A few moments later the shower curtain was pushed to the side, "I always wanted to do it in the shower, what about you?" He was naked and stepping into the tub.

"No, get out; I won't do anything with you again. OUT!" I yelled again; trying to say it as strongly as I could.

"Yes you will, unless you want everybody to know that we use to do it all the time. After all as you keep saying we are not brother and sister, what would be wrong with it? I will say you begged for it, do you think you will have any friends then." He placed his hands on my breast, "Oh yeah! You have gotten bigger little sister."

"You wouldn't do that what about your friends?" I tried to move his hands but he was still bigger and stronger than me.

"They will think I am really cool, having sex in grade school. That's the kind of friends I have. It just might be fun to tell anyway." He pushed me against the wall. I tried as hard as I could to push him back with no luck.

"See I am stronger now than I use to be. You remember my little lessons I would give you, well now they will be worse than ever." He pushed me harder and did just what he wanted to do to me.

As he was getting dressed he reminded me to keep my mouth shut or everyone will know what I did when I was younger, I might even get a broken leg or arm.

I told him he raped me, he could go to jail for that. He laughed, "You left the door unlocked for me to come in." Then he left.

I stayed in the shower and scrubbed every inch of my body five times and still felt dirty. I wasn't a little kid any more, I knew it was wrong. But, no way did I want anyone to know what had happened then or now. I will just have to make sure we were never alone again.

This I was able to do, I even talked my little sister into sleeping with me a lot of the time. We would lie in bed and play games until we fell asleep. I would feel safer when she was with me, I felt like I could sleep. Even if she was small and couldn't do anything, it made me feel better. Mom would ask why she was sleeping with me; I just told her she was afraid of being alone. That seemed to take care of it.

As hard as I tried, it wasn't good enough. One day my step-brother was to be gone all day, so I could relax. However, he came back saying his plans had changed and we would have the whole afternoon to ourselves. I told him no way, I had a boyfriend that could beat the shit out of him. Bill, really wasn't my boyfriend, but I felt I needed to say something.

"If you're talking about the sailor up the street, you've got to be joking. He is too old; you are just a kid to him." He started to walk towards me. He may be bigger than me, but I was faster than him. I made it out the front door before he could reach me. I spent the day with a friend until mom got home. Luckily for me, he was gone when I came home. From then on, I really had to be careful.

It seems things just go from bad to worse. My sister and I were sleeping in my room when noise coming from the living room woke me up. I crept out of bed to see what was going on. The kitchen light was on and I could make out three figures in the middle of the living room. A man sitting in a chair; a woman kneeled in front of him (it was my mom), and another man on the floor behind her. They were all naked; I couldn't believe what I was seeing. I couldn't believe she would do something like this in our home. I flipped on the overhead light; they all stopped and looked up at me, shock all over their faces. "What the hell is going on here? What if my baby sister was to come out here and see this?" I was so mad I was shaking all over, not from fear but anger.

"Get back to bed and stay there," Mom said. She was really drunk.

"NO, you get them out of here right now or I will start screaming I'll even go outside and scream. Get them out now." Mom could tell I meant every world I said.

"OK, go to your room and I'll take them away, go back to your room." She stood up; I had never seen her without something on. Even at her age she was a very good looking woman. She had very little body fat on her and still had those long beautiful legs.

"Hurry I want them out." I turned and walked away, but didn't go to my room. I didn't want to wake my sister up. Instead, I went into Mom's room. Crawling onto her bed was easy since it was one step inside the door. It was an oversized king bed. It was pushed up against the wall. With the dresser in the room, you could hardly get around the bed. I lay there waiting for the front door to open and close. I wondered why no one else had woken up and came to see what was happening. I was glad that my sister didn't, but she is a sound sleeper and very little woke her up.

Finally the door opened and closed, I let out a sigh of relief. I rolled over to go to sleep. Then the bedroom light flipped on and standing in the doorway was one of the men from the living room. He was dressed only in his underpants. I could tell from the way he was swaying and his eyes half open that he was very drunk.

"There you are pretty little girl. I was looking for you." His words were very slurred. I didn't move, I couldn't move. "Your mother is taking my friend home and will be back to get me." He was working his way around the bed towards me.

I jumped right out of that big bed. Oh please don't let my little sister wake up, I kept thinking. Quickly I went to the living room and sat in a chair in the corner, thinking it would be safe. Why wasn't either of my brothers waking up; are they dead? Fear hit me, were they dead? I tried to call out but no sound came from my mouth.

The man came out and stood next to the chair. "Don't be afraid I won't hurt you. I only want to get to know you." He kneeled by the chair putting his hand on my leg. "Your skin is so smooth and soft" he muttered, moving his hand up my leg.

Why did I have to wear a nightgown tonight? I was safe when my sister was sleeping with me. Now I must keep her safe; nobody was going to hurt her. That thought motivated me into action. I jumped right out of the chair and heading for the kitchen before he could stand up. I was lucky he was so drunk. *Look around, find something, anything.* I was thinking when I spotted a large knife in the drainer; grabbing it just as he reached the kitchen door. "There is the door, get out!" I held up the knife so he could clearly see it. "I will use this!"

He stopped in the doorway. "I need to get my clothes on." Keeping his eyes on the knife, he took one step back.

"Get out now or you will see just how sharp this really is." I reached for another knife sitting in the drain, it wasn't as big, but I felt two were better than one. "Get out! I will throw the clothes out to you." I took one small step towards him.

Out he went; I rushed over to the door and locked it. I had been holding the first knife so hard that it took a moment to loosen my grip on it. I could hear him calling me to give him his clothes. I gathered them up and squeezed them out through a crack in the door opening, then quickly relocked it. There, I leaned against the door, trying to calm down.

Dead; are they dead? Moving to my step-brother's room, I thought I would be glad if he was dead. Opening the door seeing him lying on his bed I couldn't tell; then he moved. A little disappointed, I closed the door. I checked on my younger brother, he was alive too. Then to my room where my sister was thankfully, sleeping like a baby. I walked over very quietly and covered her up. I went back to the living room and waited for my mom to come back. When she did she was so drunk she could hardly walk. She didn't even see me; just stumbled to her bedroom, dropped on her bed and was out.

I just wanted to yell at her, wanted to tell her she was a bad mother. I hated her. I never had the nerve to talk about this with her and she never brought it up either. There I was, with a father who wasn't my father, who hated me, and did whatever he could to make my life hell; with a brother who wasn't my brother, but was hell himself. He had made me hate myself. Then there were the younger half brother and sister that had no worries or cares. I just hoped they would be spared any pain. Lastly, there was Mother, a drunk who left a man in our home to rape me. Did I mean so little to her? Where did that leave me?

Chapter Five

The next day I felt as though I'd been beaten-up; I could hardly move. There were so many thoughts coming and going; I couldn't get a hold on even one. In a zombie-like state, I walked around, getting dressed, brushing my teeth and combing my hair. There was no way I could go to school and told my mom. When she asked why, I wanted to yell at her because of what I'd seen her do the night before. Instead, I said I'd had bad dreams all night; which in a way was true. I didn't get any sleep and felt sick. So, she called the school to report my absence.

After I was alone in the house I couldn't sit, stand, or lay down for more than a minute. There was nobody I could talk to, except one person. I didn't know if he was even home; I will go see, anything was better than standing around here. If his car was there, so was he. In fact he was up and working on that car. When I told him I needed to talk, he could see how upset I was. He laid down his tools and put his arms around me. I don't know how long we stood like that. He said we could go into the house, his sister was gone and her baby was sleeping. We sat at the kitchen table just looking at each other; I didn't know how to start. I had never told him much about my past, just bits and pieces here and there; if he had guesses at more he never said so. I finally started, and when I did I couldn't stop until the events of the whole night were out.

"How could any mother do something like that? She has no right being a mother." He reached across the table and took my hands in his and looked right into my eyes. "You did right, I am proud of you. What finally gave you the strength to stand up for yourself?"

I hadn't been able to think right let alone know what or where that girl from last night had come from. "I don't know, I think I was so scared that something would happen to my sister. I have always worried about her; I want her to be safe."

"Patty;" he stepped in front of me and raised me up to stand in front of him. "Patty, I want you to listen to me, you need to hear me. YOU ARE YOUR SISTER. You need to worry about you. You need to keep yourself safe. Hear me; you are so much better than that family of yours. Stand up to them; don't let them bring you down with them. Don't let anyone ever bring you down; don't let anyone ever use you. You have that right; but, only you can make it happen."

He kissed me like he was afraid he would break me. He hugged me and asked if I felt better. Yes I did, I was thinking again. I was thinking again and there were so many thoughts. Then the baby started to cry so Bill went and got him. We took the baby outside and watched Bill work on his car until his sister got home. I kissed Bill and thanked him for listening to me. It was time to go home.

After sitting at home alone with my thoughts I knew what I had to do, what I was GOING to do. As soon as my step-brother got home and went to his room, I knew it was now or never.

I went to my step-brother and I told him what had happened with the man, never telling him how I found mother and the men or what they were doing, he had no right, she wasn't his mother.

"He must have been one drunken man to let a little girl like you run him off." He started laughing.

I raised my hand showing the same knife I had the night before. He grew quite. "I swear, if you ever touch me again, I will kill you. I will wait until you are sleeping and you will never wake up again." I turned to go.

"I'll tell everyone about you," he said, trying to stand tall.

I turned around still holding the knife in front of me and answered, "Then I will have to kill you. You WILL NOT TOUCH me; you WILL NOT TELL ANYONE! Do you understand?" I could feel all the hate and anger pouring out of me. It seemed to hit home and was really scaring him. I hope he believed me; I meant every word I said.

He did, "Yes, just get out and stay away from me." The fear was very evident on his face.

It felt good being in the driver seat and I remember thinking, *I hope he wet his pants.* I smiled and left. He never bothered me again. He moved out to live with a friend two weeks later. That was the last I'd ever see of him.

Strength

I felt a light breeze across my face. Could it be there?

I throw a pebble in to the water and it makes small ripples.
Could it be?

I see a group of children laughing and smiling. If I try that
will I find it?

While weeding, I see a small evergreen reaching above to get
a peek of sunlight. This plant has to have it.

I fear that if I don't find it I won't be able to go on.

It is here all around me, I just need to put out my hand, know
I have a need and then accept it.

2-17-1975

Chapter Six

My step-brother was out of my life; my step-father was out of my life. Finally, I no longer had to worry about being alone. Life had become quite and safe for me. I had met a young man who was treating me the way I had always dreamed of being treated. The past was in the past, somewhere in the back of my mind. I had also found something wonderful, courage to stand up for myself.

Bill had said things to me that morning I had never heard of or thought about before. I was worried about my little sister because that's what I really wanted for myself. The other was that I had the right. I never realize I had the right before. Bill would build on these ideas for the next year and half. I really felt that I had found my 'white knight'.

My best friend, Barbie, and I would walk around our block and talk, dream up make-believe worlds where we both could be happy. It's true, likes draw likes, she never talked about her secret life and I never talked about mine, we just accepted each other. One day while walking, we met a young sailor stationed closed by. He spent weekends staying at his sister's house to work on his car. This house was three doors from mine. Like typical teenage girls, Barbie and I would make sure we showed up when he was working on his car.

We would talk to him and even try to help him with is car. He was eighteen, I was fourteen and Barbie was thirteen. I really thought he was cute and a man of the world, although he really hadn't seen much more than we had. He got use to us coming around and seemed to enjoy our company. One weekend Barbie and I were unable to visit him and the following weekend he said he really missed our help. I began to visit him both days of the weekends without Barbie. She couldn't go out on Sundays, a family day. Bill said that he will be coming in on Friday afternoon the next week if I wanted to help him. Sure I wanted to help, or maybe really wanted to spend time with him.

The next Friday I headed for Bill's right after school. He was working on his car already. We worked on his car, and talked, he was always telling stories of the guys on his ship, what they did, their girl problems, and on and on. It was getting dark and we didn't notice the dark clouds moving in. The skies opened up and starting to pour. He said jump into the car, so I did and we were completely drenched. He turned on the radio and we sat there and talked about ourselves and our lives. I didn't tell him too much about myself. There we were sitting in his car and the radio playing, the next thing I knew he was kissing me. He pushed back, said he was sorry it just happened. I told him I wasn't in fact I was glad about it. He must have thought so too because he kissed me again.

"I know you're younger than someone I should be drawn to but I am, I think you are a very special girl." He reached into the backseat for a towel and wiped my face. "I like you but I think maybe we should be just friends, at least for now."

I didn't quit understand it but agreed with him. We sat there another half an hour or so, until the rain slowed down. It was time for me to go, he hugged me and said he would see me tomorrow and to bring Barbie too. I think I floated all the way home, then my step-brother brought me down.

This is how I would spend my week-ends and Bill was coming home on Fridays more often. I hated to go home to the hell I was living in there. It was four months after meeting Bill that my mother had brought those men home. After telling him about what happened, it brought us closer together. He was more attentive and would kiss me when I got to his house, even in front of Barbie. After my step-brother moved out, Bill would come over and we would watch a movie. He would always ask permission to put his arm around me, saying he never wanted me to think that he didn't respect me, or that he expected more from me. In a way this bothered me, I had never knew a boy who didn't want more, that's why I didn't have boyfriends. He always treated me like I was special. He once told me that most of the men on his ship would go on leave and spend every night with a different girl, he then explained that those girls would never become a wife, men didn't married that kind of girl.

It seemed he would never be finished with his car. Every weekend he had to fix something on it and even replaced the motor when he had a week leave. So we spent our time working on the car and watching movies. Once in a while I would have dinner with him and his sister's family. They were nice and friendly to me. I really thought I found the person I would marry when I got out of school. Things at home were relatively quiet except for the few times mom would come home with a man. I told Bill that I wish my sister wasn't living there, I still feared for her. He would always say that I had the strength for myself and for her.

My brother and sister would visit their father every two weeks. During one visit he asked if they wanted to live with him, since he had gotten a bigger house; but both refused. As I thought about it, I knew he really wanted a babysitter. I started thinking that maybe my sister would be safer there than with us. It took some convincing but my sister finally agreed to live with her father. I felt better, thinking she was safe from some strange man. Bill agreed with me. Now it was just my mom, my younger brother and I left at home. My younger brother and I had very little in common. Where he was very popular and cute, I was a loner and not real cute. Life was better. My time was spent with Bill, my brother doing his own thing and it seemed mom had found a man. She was still working nights and drinking but not as much.

You could see it coming. Bill's ship was leaving port. He wasn't sure where it was going but he would be gone for some time. He only had one day to spend at home, so he took me out to dinner, my first real date. We agreed to write and wait for each other. Off he went, leaving me his navy ring. I still have that ring but Bill never came back. It seems his ship was hit; he didn't live through it. I'm not really sure how I made it through but I did, although I was withdrawing again. Barbie was the reason I didn't completely leave this world. She wouldn't leave me alone, encouraging me do things we had always done before we met Bill. As time passed the sorrow subsided, but things he had given me are still with me. If I was ever to marry it would be a man like him. I would never let a person touch me unless we were married. I had the right to stand up for myself.

Chapter Seven

L ife moved on, quietly, Mom and her man became closer, my brother got into sports at school so was home very little, and I was home or with Barbie. I had just finished my tenth grade in school; we were starting summer vacation when mom gave us her news. This man, George, was in the air force and buying a house by the base. My brother and I were moving too. This time it was fine with me, but my brother wasn't happy. Moved we did, it was a small town outside of where we were living, the schools were altogether, the classes were small, mostly kids whose parent was in the air force. Mom helped my brother get on the school's baseball team, so he was happier. Mom gave me carte blanche to decorate my room any way I wanted, anything I wanted, so began my love for decorating. George seemed like a very nice man, playing catch with my brother and taking him to ball games. He would help me move furniture around and take me to get things for my room. One thing he did was get me a door knob that I could lock, that made me feel safer.

We lived in that house for one year, when George came home and announced he was being transferred to San Francisco. He wanted to marry our mother, would we have any objections. We had none. It sounded exciting. So they were married and we moved together as a family. There we both were to find a life we had never known. Mom stayed home, she had cut her drinking down to week-ends. George took a big interest in my brother's and my life, our school work, where we went, and what we wanted to do in the future. He also tried to make us act more like brother and sister. We shouldn't let other people hurt or talk about the other. It didn't take long before both of us loved and respected George. Since I didn't know my real father and hated my step-dad I asked George if I could call him my father. This made him very happy.

I have had for as long as I can remember headache and bad dreams. Most the time they didn't trouble me much, that started to change. My headache started hurting so bad that I would stand in my room and bang my head against the wall to try and stop them. This is the time my dreams, or night-meres, started to get worse, so bad I became afraid to fall asleep. I never told anybody about how often I was having them. Mom and George knew I was having some because I would wake them up screaming. I would spend most my week-ends in my room, resting as much as I could. It was at this time I learned that if I wanted something bad enough I could get it.

On day I was laying on my bed wishing I could just leave my body and mind behind somewhere and sleep without dreaming. As if it were magic it happened! I left my body and was up in the air looking down at myself. The window was open and no screen so out I went. I flew all over the base, seeing things I had not seen yet. Then I was in my body again, I didn't believe I'd really flown, but dreamed it up. I didn't care either way if I slept without bad dreams. I was able to do this over and over, floating high above everything and nothing could touch me, and I was free. I was still not sleeping at night, and the few hours of sleep I got on the week-ends wasn't enough. My body was wearing out, I was sick more than not, missing a lot of school. Mom finally took me to the doctor to find out what was wrong.

The doctor said my body was rebelling the lack of sleep. Stomach ulcers developing and my blood pressure was up too high. He wanted to know why I wasn't sleeping. So, with mom out of the room I told him that I had dreams that really scared me and was afraid to sleep. When I woke up I wouldn't remember them just that they were very scary. He gave me sleeping pills that would make me sleep and not dream, along with another medicine and I was to see a therapist. So therapy began.

During this time I started to learn and remember some of the things that happened when I was young. I was even starting to remember bits and pieces of my dreams. The pill, the understanding and the ability to stop and wake up when the dreams did start, was how I became better physically. But I had missed too much school, so it looked like I would have to do the twelfth grade over. This I would do in another state, dad was going to Viet Nam.

Once we moved again, I didn't continue therapy just went to school where I wanted to become an A student. I studied all the time to do my best. I had found one girlfriend who I would spend the night with sometimes. She too lived on base and when mom come home drunk (which she was doing more and more now that George was gone), I would go over to Shelly's house. It was through Shelly that I would meet David. He was the same age as me, but already in college. He seemed very nice, so I went out with him. He was also very smart and I enjoyed spending time with him and he was always the gentleman. We were seeing more and more of each other. I was seeing Bill in him; maybe I was lucky enough to find love twice. David said he loved me and wanted to get married when I finished school, and I agreed. Mom was very upset and said George would be angry. I didn't care; I felt that George would forgive me. We were married three days after graduation.

Chapter Eight

L ife was going to be great, like a fairytale. Four months after we were married, I found that I was pregnant. I was very excited but afraid of what David would think. At first he seemed worried, but within half an hour he, too, was excited. Towards the end of the pregnancy, David thought it would be best for us to move in with his mother so I wouldn't be left alone for long periods of time. He was going to school and working nights. I liked his mother and I did have questions about what was happening to my body that she seemed to understand.

I was having nightmares again, but of a different kind. I wondered if other women had bad dreams when they were pregnant. The dreams were crazy, like having a baby with no arms or legs. Or, what kind of legacy I was handing down to the child. The doctor would ask questions about David's and my backgrounds. There was no problem answering about David's. My mom just said she knew nothing of her family, and my birth father was out of the question. This was the first time I had ever asked her about herself and she didn't want to talk about it. The only thing she could say was that my father was of Irish descent and her background was half American Indian and half some Europe country. According to her, her family was circus people and thieves. There was really no medical information available.

The baby was born in winter and was very healthy. Two months later, we rented our place. Life seemed like it was the way it should always be except, for one thing. David's attitude toward me began to change. Love making seemed to be few and far between. That wasn't a problem for me since I never really enjoyed it anyway. In other ways, he seemed to be happy and was always home when he wasn't working or going to school. I was lost in the happiness of caring for my new baby.

He graduated from college later that year and landed a good job. First, though, it meant that he would be traveling for a year, training for the job. The baby and I went with him, staying in hotel rooms but we made it through. However, more and more he acted differently than the man I first fell in love with. He didn't want me to go anywhere, spend any money, or have any friends. His feeling was that he and the baby should be all I needed.

Right after he finished his training, we moved to his first job and found a place to rent. Once again, I was pregnant. When David found out, he changed and started treating me like I was a queen, like it was when we first got married.

After this baby was born, he changed again. He wanted to isolate me, staying home and not seeing anyone else. He had to have a complete account of every penny I spent. Then he started stopping at bars after work three or four times a week. Luckily, there was a great lady who lived across the street who would come over to help with the children, teach me more about cooking, and just be a friend when I needed one. She helped me make it through the next two years.

Pregnancy number three and again he reverted back to treating me as if I were a queen. Our best times seemed to be when I was pregnant. After each baby was born, he went back to his odd behavior toward me. My thought was, "What am I doing wrong?" I felt like a prisoner with a guard who expected me to service him from time to time.

Now there were three children. We needed a bigger place and David felt that it was time to buy our own house. Once we bought the house, he was away more than ever, spending six days or nights at the bar. If I needed anything I'd have to go there to talk to him or see him. He was always home on Sundays, in a bad mood, mad at everyone, and the children and I wished he wasn't there. It seemed there was no winning with him.

Once we went to visit David's aunt who owned a farm. The children had a great time learning how to pump water just to get it to the house, the outdoor toilet, and the animals. They learned farm life was very different then living in the city. We spent the night with all of us in one room. We had one bed and the children had the other. It wasn't bad except the beds were pushed up against the walls. My fears surfaced and I was afraid to be confined on the inside of the bed. I begged David to let me sleep on the outside, but he wouldn't have it.

And there, in mind, I could envision a sight that made me want to scream. It was my first step-father, leaning over me! In my mind's eye I could see him putting his big, fat hands all over me. I kept trying to move, but I was against the wall and there was nowhere to go!

Then it was over, and I awoke under the kitchen table, tucked in the far corner. That's where David's Uncle found me. I was crying and shaking badly. He went to get David to help. David's reaction was anger that he had to get out of bed so early, and disgusted that I was acting so childish. He didn't understand my feelings, just kept telling me it was a bad dream and to get over it. There would be no consolation from him.

Ten years after my first baby was born, I gave birth to my last baby. Though unhappy, I knew I couldn't manage four children on my own, so I had to stay married. Writing helped me. I would write what ever came to mind, taking time every morning before anyone got up to write. I was learning a lot about myself and what I wanted to do with my life. So, that filled my spare time for the next few years.

I wanted to get a job, but David was adamantly against it! When my last child began school, I insisted that I was going to work outside our home and David finally allowed me to get a part-time job. That's when I learned that all husbands were not like mine and that all wives were not slaves. Unhappiness was growing in me every day.

Finally, Judy's words about mind control were beginning to make sense to me. David had me convinced that I wasn't able to take care of myself, let alone the children. That was his way of controlling me. When our oldest child became a teenage, she started giving us trouble, as most teenagers do. David was very angry and realized he couldn't control her the way he wanted to. He gave me an ultimatum, "It's me or the child, we both can't live here." To his astonishment, I made my choice. The marriage was wrong and had to end, not just for me, but the children, too. It was my children who gave me the strength to make the right decision.

Chapter Nine

L ife was not easy, with holding down a full-time job and
being home to care for the children, but I loved it. The
older ones helped with the younger ones. They seemed to
understand that we all needed to pitch in and help to make
it work. I started to take a good look at my life, and thought
it looked good at that point. My "baggage" was still buried
deep. My feeling was that alcohol was the problem. Between
my mother, my step-father and my husband, I decided to
just stay away from drinkers.

I enjoyed my job and found I was very good at it. This
would be my career for a long time to come. With my job
and child support, we were able to live moderately. The
oldest child had finished school and had moved in with a
friend. It was time to do something for myself. Although
I had the other children with me, I was still lonely. Square
dancing turned out to be something that was fun for the
whole family. It was where I met a man who I thought was
a really good person. We became partners, he met the kids,
they all seemed to get along, and he didn't drink. When the
subject of sex surfaced, I let him know that it was something
that belonged in a marriage. So, again I took the plunge. After
four months, the reality came to light that non-drinkers had

problems, too. Soon, he became very controlling over all of us. Since I wasn't going through that again, the marriage ended very quickly. With this experience, I realized it was best to wait for all the children to grow up before I decided to date again.

Introspection began again and it was time for me to examine my baggage. This turned out to be a very difficult task. I pulled out all my old writings and started reading, really reading. So much hurt and pain! I was allowing myself to feel it, not just write and forget. At times I just wanted to quit, but I didn't. How could these things have been real? The horror seemed too much for someone to endure. How could I ever have forgotten? The writings allowed me to see deep inside and painfully brought the memories. It was almost like physical pain.

I knew deep inside my step-father played a big part in my feelings, and the way I precede life. Shortly after I'd married David, I wrote,

> *"A little girl sitting on a curb asks, "Why does love hurt?"*
>
> *You smile at her and say, "Love doesn't hurt; it heals."*
>
> *Big green eyes look up and ask, "Why does love make you sad?"*
>
> *Again you smile and reach for the frail little hand, and say, "Love is happiness and it is wonderful."*

Now with a tear in her eye, she asks, "Why does love bring such loneliness and why does it leave such a big scar?"

You wipe her eyes and for the first time see the deep emptiness there and say, "Love builds you up and gives you much to look forward to."

You feel like putting your arms around this small, pretty child, but she backs away, so you ask, "Where did you learn about love?"

She looks down and in a voice that becomes so quiet, it is hard to hear.

She speaks only two words, "My dad."

As she walks away you see God's hands around her, but still you don't understand.

Although the truth hurts, I knew it was time to face it, time to see all the ugliness that had been my life. The hate, the hurt, the pain and the guilt I felt; all those monsters had to be confronted. My shame came between me and the things I desired. Now I understood why sex was so distasteful, why I couldn't stand anyone's touch, why I didn't trust easily and why I couldn't watch certain movies or read certain books. I favored fantasy so much and longed for a different life and world. Now I thought the healing and understanding would start, and life would begin to change. I believed I was free. Sadly, I hadn't dug deep enough.

My youngest child was a senior in high school when I met the next man who would become my husband. He was the kindest man I'd known beside Bill and my father, George.

Yes, he had problems and was the first to talk about them and what he was doing to handle them.

He was a Vietnam Vet with Post Traumatic Stress syndrome. He was monitored by a doctor and on medication to help control his disorder. He was the commander of the local VFW, working at the hospital, and spending time with his mother who suffered from Alzheimer's disease. He was kind and giving, and peopled liked him. We were married and for two years life was great. He had enough money coming which allowed me to finally stop working. I, too, joined the VFW and became active with them. We spent all of our time together and he even enjoyed babysitting the grandchildren with me.

We were living in my house that I alone was paying for. He convinced me to pay off the mortgage and then get a home improvement loan so we could fix up the house. When the mortgage was paid off, his name was added to the title on the house. We started improving the home, having a great time together. Friends were coming over for parties, dinners, or whatever. Life was good; I had no worries, except for the same old nightmares. Why were they still there; hadn't I accepted what happened to me and believed the blame was not mine? Robert would hold me and tell me everything would be alright. He also suggested that I talk to someone about them.

I started to see Linda, a psychotherapist. Linda told me that even though I had come to terms with the things that happened to me, there were many feelings, thoughts, and beliefs that I was unaware of and had not dealt with. My dreams were trying to tell me there was still more work to do. So it began; more writing and more questions.

Much of how we are shaped is developed when we are young. So much of the information I'd been given was wrong. It was hard to know what was right. I thought I knew right from wrong, and tried to do right. Linda helped me to understand what I wanted for myself, how to take care of me, how I wanted others to treat me. Once we began digging in, I began to understand what she was telling me. She showed me I didn't believe I deserved the right things that other people had. Those were changes in my thinking that had to be accomplished.

She explained that I was still blaming myself for everything that happened, that somehow I was at fault. "You should have faced both your first step-father and your mother." This was no longer possible since they were both dead. We played acted, it was hard and painful, but, I began to feel better. It was much easier to make a list of what seemed to be wrong with me as opposed to what was right with me! My list of what I thought life should be was so out of whack; it was a wonder I ever made the right decisions for myself. Changing everything one believes is a very slow process. First, you have to tear it all down, throw it all away, burn it or bury it. Not easy, but rebuilding is even harder.

The year I was seeing Linda, Robert was supportive the best way he knew how. We agreed that I should go to college, something I'd always wanted to do. I was learning new and exciting things and really enjoyed it. Then things started to happen at home. My visits to Linda were once every two months now. Robert began to act strange.

Robert decided he also wanted to attend college. He stopped taking his medication to achieve this. He began to get paranoid about things, things I couldn't understand. Because of doctor-patient confidentiality, she would not discuss his condition with me. In the end, he stole a semi-truck and landed in jail. The only way he could get out was to admit himself to the Veteran's Hospital, which he did. Unfortunately, his mental state was so deteriorated that he didn't trust the doctors or nurses and checked out of the hospital. He also didn't trust me. Once again, I ended up in divorce court. On my own again, deep in debt; lost my home and just enough understanding of myself to get in trouble again. But to be all fair, he did make it possible for me to go to college.

Chapter Ten

Six months on my own and the downward spiral began. Would I ever learn? I was still attending school and had gotten a night-time job trying to make ends meet. My nest was empty, I could no longer afford to see Linda and the loneliness crept in. I desperately needed someone to communicate with.

Along came Chris, who professed to have been an abused child, although not in the same way as it had been for me. We were on the same wavelength and had really good conversations. He helped me confirm my feelings. He turned out to a very good liar. He was employed, so it wasn't until we were married that I found out he was living off his brother and had big debts of his own. With school finished, I had a science degree and yes, another divorce under my belt.

How could one person fall for so much "wrong"? After working with Linda, I thought I was on the right road. She did tell me there were things that still needed to be unraveled. It was up to me to find them and turn my life into what I wanted it to be. What could be missing? I just wanted to be happy, and have someone who really loved me. I thought that was what everyone wanted.

Through Linda I learned to love myself before I could love someone or be loved by someone. I realized that I was defining love for myself through others, if I had someone who loved me than I could love myself, too. I needed others to tell me I was good and I was smart. I didn't have the confidence to realize it in my own mind. Understanding about the abuse did not seem to help me move on and be able to have a normal sex life.

My children bless their hearts, started to worry about me. They knew I was unhappy. They were watching my every move; it seemed they wanted to know everywhere I went, everyone I was with. They were driving me crazy. One time, I was in the yard cleaning and didn't hear the phone. The oldest child calls the next child, who didn't know where I was, nor did the last two. When I came inside and saw so many calls, I made a call to the oldest. They were actually thinking about calling the police because I was missing. Was I really acting that badly, was there something going on with me that made them fear for me? Things were going to have to change, but how.

Everywhere I went I was reminded of all the wrong decisions I had made, all the places I used to go to hide from the world. Somehow, I needed to get away from all of it, go someplace that was new, and try to start over.

So, I moved fifteen hundred miles away from everything and everyone I knew. I was able to transfer with my job, and except for the pictures of the children and information I had gathered on my real father and my mother's families. I gave mostly everything else away. I kept just enough furniture and personal items which fit into a ten-foot truck. Before I left, there was one thing I could never bring myself to do.

I had to really bury Bill forever; I didn't need any ghosts coming with me. I wrote him a long letter, crying the whole time. Yes, I was really able to cry now. I took the letter and his ring, went to the park and buried them both, said my good-byes and left town. I never looked back.

On My Own

The time comes, when you ask how do you pick up the threads of your life. You tell yourself it is over, time and time again. All is dead, that you can forget, set it aside. But, then you find yourself right back where you started, the hurt, pain, distrust, and the feelings of being lost. It is not until you finally realize that you can never truly forget, go back to make things right.

There are some wounds that wrap themselves around your heart, that become a part of your very bone, they have taken hold of you until you die and then they go on.

When you understand that you must move on. Knowing that some things can never heal; never let go of its hold on you. It is when you decide to embrace the hurt, pain, and isolation it brings.

Decide to use that which is truly a part of you. Use it to overcome, to make you what your heart tells you who you truly are and want to be. The battle can end; the life can begin.

19-5-1999

Chapter Eleven

The changes were happening; new apartment and new job. It would take time to get used to all the new changes, but I wasn't in a hurry. It took me more than a year to learn to walk, so I wanted to give myself time to learn in which direction I was heading.

Heading toward the right direction was going to be a tough road to find. There would be hard times and some wrong turns, but this time I wasn't going to accept and stand still. Even if I just stumbled over them, I need to feel and believe I can make the changes. I needed to feel it and believe it. Being by myself and learning to be alone and independent would be the next change in my life.

I continued to write, dreaming I'd write that great novel that sold a million copies. That would really help my budget and pay my bills. The problem was I'd get a good idea and start really strong. Within a few weeks, I just couldn't move the story any further. Writer's block? Then another idea would come and another block. I couldn't keep my mind moving forward. Was I writing about the wrong subjects? I needed to write about what I knew, what I had lived.

Sure, I could write my "life story"; but would anyone really want to read it? Where did I start? When I tried to write about one thing, my mind would be on something else. Maybe I wasn't meant to be a writer after all. In the end, I just wrote the way I always did, writing what I felt not what I thought I should be writing. The hope always lingered in the back of my mind that someday I would find the book in me.

Outside of trying to be a writer, I still needed to work on me. I received a promotion at work which meant more money and being in charge of other employees. Who would have believed it? Taking charge of my own life was challenge enough. Now I'd be taking charge of others! The business aspect was easy, but I was still fighting my personal issues.

My boss was a great guy, he pulled me into his office one day, to my surprise said, "Pattie, I know you have only been with us three months, but I believe you have what it takes to make things happen." He looked at me and smiled.

"I try to do the best I can. I really enjoy my job," was all I could think of saying. He informed me that he had been in touch with my prior supervisor, who had only good things to say about me and the work I performed. At that moment I felt I was flying high on myself. Forget the work I needed to do on myself.

"We would like to offer you a position in our management team." He handed me the information on the new position and the new wages. I was thrilled. At last, the opportunities were surfacing. He informed me that everybody would be glad to help me out while I was learning the ropes. Was I ready for this? I wasn't sure, but knew I would give it my best shot. I told myself it was the new me.

I was a fast learner and a hard worker, and was beginning to feel that I could do the job. "I can keep this separate from my personal life and feelings." I said it over and over enough times that I believed it. I needed to learn to juggle both work and life together.

To start, I thought about what made a good manager. Using my past experience from managers I had known, the good and the bad. It seemed that I was doing a good job in making the right decisions. *Why couldn't I do the same in my life?* The job had two sides, like a two-way street. I was learning how to give and also learning to expect certain things in return. After two months, I was again called into my boss' office.

"You're doing a great job; your people are coming to me to report how well you're doing." He put out his hand to shake mine and said, "Keep up the good work."

"Deal," I shook back. When I left his office, it seemed I'd been in that place before. It would come to me later that year.

It had been a tough time. Learning to deal with work and making progress with my personal life. Dealing with work was the easy part. Working on me was the tough part. Taking two steps forward and then one back; I wonder if I would ever make any progress. It would do good to treat my life like I treated work.

Chapter Twelve

A lthough I was able to keep my personal life separate from work, I couldn't keep work from my personal life.

I was beginning to expect returns for what I put into it. Not only was my job a two way street, so was my life becoming a two way street. I was starting to give back to myself. When I did well, I now could accept and embrace it. Realization that I wasn't to blame was clear. When my children told me I was a good mother, the best in the world, I felt proud. I could do things well and I started to like myself. I was someone I wanted to spend time with. All the bad feelings and bad things I'd been led to believe were disappearing.

I began painting again, seeing the beauty in what I created. Also, decorating was a great hobby of mine and friends asked me to help them decorate their homes. Step by step, I was moving forward, seeing how far I'd come and what I wanted to do next. My life became happier not because of some event, but because of how I was feeling about myself. Could this be one of the missing parts that Linda was talking about?

My social life expanded by spending time with some of the ladies from work. Being with a group I felt safe and comfortable. It was nice getting out and dancing, not with any commitments, just for fun. It was time to take things slow. I still had good and bad days, and wondered if I'd ever find peace.

My writing became more introspective and detailed. I was looking deep inside, not always liking what I saw. At times it hurt so much I wanted to just stop but knew I shouldn't. I learned to accept that I was human and not an angel. Linda gave me tools to work with, making lists of good and bad. Finally, the bad list was getting harder to write where the good was becoming easier. Progress was becoming evident.

At this point, loneliness set in now and then, but I was smart enough not to think about getting involved. People enjoyed being around me, and seemed to be delighted by my sense of humor and my brain. Life was fun and I enjoyed what I was creating. This was real life, not fantasy. Part of me was still dreaming of a happily ever after.

With the changes taking place in me, I wondered if the people who knew me before would recognize me now. Did that really matter or was I just trying to feel good about myself because others around me felt good about me? Maybe to some extent, but I wanted them to see me happy, especially those that made an effort to help me. Wouldn't it be great to say, "See I made it out and now I can fly." Then the chance came, I got time off and headed back home to visit my children and grandkids.

My children seemed amazed at how I looked, I was younger now. They couldn't believe how much I smiled and laughed. My old friends said much the same adding I was more open and very funny. When I visited my former co-workers, they seemed truly happy seeing me. Some wanted me to vow to keep in touch; although I agreed, I knew I probably wouldn't. The past was going to stay in the past; the goal was to keep moving forward. Now I was taking three or four steps forward and only one back.

After returning home I was feeling brave, and decided to venture out on my own, without my safety team. The VFW, seemed a safe bet. It was. Everybody seemed friendly, asking me questions about myself. Now I took pride in talking about myself. This was a place I could go on my own and feel relaxed, like a teenager finally old enough to go out.

Each time I visited the VFW, I made more and more friends. Even the guys were paying attention to me and I was asked to dance frequently. I really liked to dance, but tried to keep some distance. Everyone was very nice and nobody pushed for more than I showed I was willing to give. They were making me feel safer than I wanted to admit I was.

One year had passed since I'd been on my own. What an accomplishment! I finally reached the turning point. My life was heading in the direction I wanted it to go. I'd come a long way, knew I still had a long way to go. For now, I was going to celebrate where I am, by eating cheesecake!

Chapter Thirteen

My first Thanksgiving and Christmas holidays were spent unpacking and getting settled in my new apartment. Starting a new job kept me busy and the holidays passed quickly.

Holidays had always been a big deal with the children, even if we didn't have much money. Everything had to be decorated inside and out. If we couldn't buy it, we made it. There was always a big dinner on Christmas Eve, even after the kids moved out. The grandkids seemed to take over the decorating. We always had a busy and good time. This year was different, I had time. Now I was alone. I was going to still make the most of it.

I went out shopping, got something for everyone and actually had a good time doing it. Nobody there to tell me it cost too much, it wasn't the right thing, or that is not what they wanted. It was fun, wrapping everything, making a card for each, and sending them off. I even put up a Christmas tree with all the decorations that the kids had made through the years. It had been at least two years since I'd decorated so they seemed like new. Nothing was going to bring me down. I rationed that I was not the only person to be alone on Christmas. Wanting to fend off any loneliness, I bought myself a gift. A puppy!

Two nights before Christmas I went to the VFW to see some friends, and since it was Saturday and there was a band, I wanted to dance. "Would you like to dance?" he asked as he bowed (just like in the old movies.) This was Wayne, a tall man, older than me, but not too old. He had a full head of salt and pepper hair.

"Yes," I replied, as he took my hand to lead me to the floor. It was country night and the band was playing a two-step song. Wayne wasn't too bad at dancing and when the dance was over he took me back to my seat. He asked if he could join me, I said it would be fine.

He said he worked at the base nearby and was doing a job that would last about two more months. He didn't seem to be in the market for a long-term relationship. I just wasn't sure if I was looking.

We were having fun, dancing almost every dance, and talking to those around us. The drinks were getting to me, and I knew I need to cut back. When it was time to go, Wayne took both of my hands, "I think I should follow you home to make sure you get there alright."

I had to admit that I thought it was a good idea. "Sure, that would be nice of you."

I was wondering what I was going to do when we reached my house. A one-night stand was not what I had in mind. All the way home I kept wondering what was I doing?

Wayne jumped out of the car and opened the door for me. He knew how to be a gentleman, which was nice. Right up to the front door I wasn't sure. Then, out of my mouth came "Would you like to come in and have one last beer?" Was this the beer or was this me speaking?

"Sure that would be nice," and he opened my front door for me.

He liked my new puppy and played with her until I brought out the beer and handed him one. This was new for me since any man I'd had inside my home was someone I was planning to marry. I was feeling a little wild didn't know if it was the drinks or just something inside of me. "Would you like to see the house?" I guess I would just see what happened.

I showed him the living room, kitchen, spare room, then said I needed to take the puppy out. He came with me. He seemed impressed with the way I had decorated the house and he loved my paintings, or maybe he was being nice.

When we were back inside, he took me in his arms and gave me a very passionate kiss. He said I hadn't shown him my bedroom. Actually, I didn't remember showing him the bedroom or not. The next thing I did remember was waking in my bed, naked and alone. I don't know if I had a good time or if he had a good time. I hoped someone did. It seemed funny, I didn't feel bad but I didn't feel good either, wonder what that meant?

After I took the puppy out and headed for the coffee, I noticed on the refrigerator was a note, written on my 'to buy' pad, *Took puppy out before I left, please call when you get up. Wayne. PS: don't forget the milk.* He had covered my word milk with a smiley face.

Now that was sweet, maybe I should call him, might find out if we had a good time. I was still feeling wild and some shame. The thought of my mother jumped into my mind. Was I going to be like her? Was I so lonely that I would throw all care out the window? I really wasn't sure what bothered me more, drinking too much or the loose sex. I knew that I could explain both away but I was trying to be true to myself, not bagging my problems. Was I over thinking everything, making problems where there weren't any. I knew I wasn't my mother. I knew I wasn't an alcoholic. So, I called. "Hello, Wayne, this is Pattie."

"Hello, and Merry Christmas. How are you feeling today?" He said, sounding very happy.

"I am fine and you?" Thinking I sounded dumb.

"No headache?" He asked.

"No, I don't get headaches or hangovers. What about you?"

"A small one; what do you have planned for Christmas day?"

"I have a long list of things to do, talk to my kids, and a stack of movies." I really was set for Christmas day.

"I will be seeing some family; would you like to join us?"

I really was fine with spending the day by myself. "No, I think I better stay close to home, the kids will be upset if they can't talk to me. But, thank you for asking."

"Well, okay, but I really want to see you again; how about dinner on Wednesday?"

"Sure, that would be nice, but it will have to be an early night, have to work Thursday." I thought it would be nice to find out what I really thought of him when I wasn't drinking. He said that would be nice and we made plans.

I did enjoy being by myself, I slept really late, played with the puppy, got four phone calls, one from each of the kids. I talked to the kids and to each grandchild. It seemed everyone was very happy with their gifts, and I told them how much I liked the ones they'd sent me. I also spent time trying to understand how I felt about Wayne and what we had done. I thought I should be ashamed, but I wasn't. Again I worried what would people think of me, how would they look at me? It was just silly, what difference did it make. I wasn't the first woman to do that nor would I be the last. It might have made it better if I could remember what we did or didn't do.

Wayne was just as I remembered him, good looking and very polite. Opening doors, pulling my chair out for me, it was nice to be treated like a lady. He told me how nice I looked, better than he remembered. Dinner was great; we talked about our jobs, my art, and construction work. He sounded like he knew what he was talking about. When dinner was over he suggested we stop by the VFW for a drink. So now I would see how others might react to me. I also reminded myself to watch the drinking.

When we arrived, there weren't a lot of people but nobody was looking at me, pointing at me, or whispering about me, if they knew, nobody cared, so why should I. We only stayed for two drinks. Nothing was said about what had happened the other night. He walked me to my door, kissed me and said "I had a great time the other night." So now I knew.

"I have two tickets to the dance club on New Year's Eve. Would you join me?" Then he kissed me again. I said I'd be happy to join him.

I had a few days to get ready, clean the house, and decide just what I really wanted to do. This time I wanted to be sure of what I wanted. I was feeling wild, free, and eager for something, not sure what. Maybe I wasn't the loner I was trying to be; maybe it was all right to need to be with another person as long as I didn't become dependent on them. Was I taking another step or fooling myself?

On New Year's Eve, Wayne was right on time and really looked nice. He was trim and firm. His hair was combed straight back which showed off the shape of his face and the dimples in each cheek. A nice gray sweater finished him off showing that he truly was slim. I was glad I took the extra time to dress up myself and that I was wearing low heels so I didn't look that much shorter than him. I decided to wear a long skirt and a lose blouse with threads of gold in it. My hair was up on top of my head, giving me more height. I even put on some make-up, not much. He said that I really looked nice and I felt like I did. This felt like a good beginning.

The club was decorated, they had a long table of food and the band was playing. We found a table for two and ordered drinks. Then we took a trip to the food table. It almost seemed like a night in Never-land. There were several friends from the VFW there too, everyone was having fun and laughing. At midnight we kissed, a long sexy kiss. I was really glad I was watching what I was consuming.

We left about 1:00 a.m. and headed for my house. As always, he opened doors for me and when he closed the front door he grabbed me and kissed me like he was never going to let me go; I didn't want him to. At that moment, the puppy had other ideas, so we took her outdoors to answer nature. When we got back inside, Wayne grabbed me again, kissing me and moving his hands to my breast. All of a sudden, I felt different, my muscles were getting tight. I knew the feeling and knew what it meant; we would have sex but I wouldn't be there. Wayne sensed that something was wrong and asked me. I said I was fine. Wayne kept telling me to relax, but I couldn't. We parted with a kiss good-bye. I knew it would be the last time I would see Wayne. I was sorry because he was so nice, but I wouldn't miss him. I really didn't feel he was a *Mr. Right*. I think I was feeling wild, because I knew we would never be more than what we were.

Although I never felt any shame for that brief fling, I did worry that something was really wrong with me. Was it physical or mental? I made an appointment with a doctor to find out. The doctor said he couldn't see anything that was physically wrong. He had seen some scarring but nothing that should cause me any trouble.

So if it wasn't physical than it had to be mental, this was just one more thing that I could thank my step-father and my step-brother for. Would I ever be normal, would I ever be able to enjoy what most women enjoyed? The biggest question was if I was going to let this take away what I had gained for myself. I had been without sex for more than three years, yet I couldn't enjoy participating in it. It seemed to be just a chore. Maybe someday I would really get over everything that happened. For now, I was going to just live life.

I spent the next five months the same as I had before Wayne. Just working, being with friends, arts and crafts, even did some more decorating. When I stopped by the VFW, I'd talk to men but never brought one home.

Friend

Friend I remember you as being Strong and protective

You have been my eyes to see this world

My brain to gain understanding

And my strength to walk on my own

But did you know that your gentle hands taught me caring

Your silent moment taught me patience

Your smiles taught me to forgive

My feet will never fill your shoes

But because of you I will walk as straight and proud as anyone.

2-10-200

Chapter Fourteen

While lunching with Nancy, a friend from work, she asked me if I would do her a favor. She and her boyfriend were taking out an old buddy of his. Although the man was older than us, half blind and hard of hearing, she was hoping I would join them, "A foursome would be better than a threesome." Wow, I thought.

"Gee it sounds like fun, can't see, can't hear, very old, think he'll make it through the night." I laughed a little and said it would be a free dinner so I would do it.

Nancy said he was nice and very funny and assured me I would have a good time. Well, I wasn't sure since I'd never been on a blind date. The plan was that I'd meet them, so if it didn't work out, I could leave.

His name was Lee, eleven years my senior, he was tall thin and had a full head of gray hair. He was a talker and he was smart. He had one story after another, each one funnier than the last. He and Nancy's boyfriend shared stories of the service. Nancy and I shared stories of work. We all had an enjoyable evening and I even stayed until everyone else was ready to leave. Lee said he'd like to see me again and asked for my phone number. I told him I didn't go out much.

"But you do eat right?" he asked

"Not much, but sure you could have my number." I wrote it down and handed it to him. "Will you be able to see that?" I asked.

"Sure I have and extra pair of eyes." He took the paper.

He called later that week and invited me to dinner. I agreed and he said, "You'll have to pick me up; they took my license away for failure to yield at a stop." He had a rough voice but it seemed to have a laugh in it.

It was quite different than what I'd been accustomed to. He leaned on me to get around, and I read the menu to him. The dinner was good and so was the conversation. Lee talked a lot about himself and what a full life he'd lead. He was in the Air force, worked for civil service and he was in the Army. He had been married three times, buried two wives and divorced one. He had four children. He also traveled around the world. He just talked and talked, which meant I didn't have to. The evening ended and I dropped him at his front gate. It was a nice night, but there is something about him that kind of niggled at the back of my mind. I wasn't sure what it was, but when he asked to see me again I agreed.

We saw each other two or three times a week, and we always enjoyed each other's company. He finally got me to talk about myself. I told him most everything from the time I was eighteen, and he was very understanding. After our fifth date, he kisses me good night. It felt a bit like kissing Daddy George, a very wired feeling.

Lee did remind me very much of my daddy George, which meant that I trusted him. Lee asked me if I could get some time off around the fourth of July. He explained that every fourth they had a big family reunion in their home town and he'd like me to go with him. He was picking up the tab, his son was coming and I'd be safe. He said I didn't have to worry about my virtue.

After securing time off from work, we were on our way. It was a nice five day vacation, and true to his word, my virtue was intact, even though we stayed in the same room. His being blind made me less self-conscious in that I never felt he was watching. He had a good family, lots of them, and they all liked each other. They were a real family and it was easy to be relaxed around them.

Once home, it was back to work and even had to put in extra time to catch up on some projects. It was a week before I saw him again. He invited me to dine at his house, and his daughter was doing the cooking. When I arrived I met his youngest daughter. She seems nice enough, but not what I had expected. She was tall like her father, on the heavy side, and definitely on the quiet side. The table was set, the meal had been prepared, and when we sat down to have dinner, his daughter left. We both cleared the table and washed the dishes. He did a good job at washing dishes. When everything was done we sat at the kitchen table and talked.

"Pattie you are a very smart lady, and fun to be with." He started. He continued with, "I would really like to take you to bed and make love to you. What do you think?"

While I was wondering when this subject was going to come up, the straight forwardness surprised me. Even though the time we spent together was enjoyable, I hadn't thought of a sexual rendezvous with him. So I said, "You

Tona Gardner

know that I have had bad experiences with men in my past. I am not sure I am ready to get into another relationship. Everyone I have been in ended badly. I have some heavy debts that I need to take care of so I work long hours. I wouldn't be able to add to a relationship right now, I couldn't work on it." At that point in time, I didn't want to concentrate on another person.

"I know that you have had a rough time and I think you are one heck of a person to come through everything and not be a bitter old lady." He contained, "I can get you out of debt."

"Even as good as it sounded; I don't ever want anyone to pay my debts." I voiced this to him. Before he could answer I added that I would have to be married in order to have a relationship again.

"I was thinking that you could move in with me, I would pay all the bills. That would leave you all your rent and utility money to put towards your debts; this would allow you to pay your bills off sooner. I would only make it possible for you to pay them off. I really understand finances, you could do it," He said.

"You are talking about me giving up my home and moving in with you, but what happens if it doesn't work out?" I needed to think, it was moving too fast. I was telling myself all along I wasn't going to get involved or married again. I started thinking that in some ways it sounded good. But, I needed to protect myself too. What was he asking? Move in with him and become his sex partner? In return I get out of debt, is it worth it? My mind was spinning. It was more than wild, it was crazy.

"The only way I'd agree to this is if we were married," I started.

Before I could say anything else he said, "Then marry me." He didn't even seem to think about what he was saying. "You will get my house, so you will have a home that is truly yours. It should be completely paid for in five years. You will be able to collect my social security which I am sure will be more than yours."

"What are we talking about here, we haven't known each other that long, you don't really know me and what I need, sometimes I get crazy. I don't know you, what you need, or if I can give it to you, how to care for your special needs." Now we were talking marriage, but, I was the one to bring it up. I didn't think he would go that far.

He said that he really enjoyed being with me, he hated being alone but hated it mostly at night. "I am still a man with a man's need." He said that he would keep having his daughter come over when I was at work; he wasn't asking me to quit work or even cut down on the time. He said that he didn't want to take away any of my freedom, I could continue as I had been living only it would be him I would sleep with. Think of it as an adventure, every day, every week we will learn new things about each other, it would put interest into our relationship. "So, what do you think?"

There was a lot to take in, a lot to think about. I wasn't going to make a quick decision; I wanted to think about this and all it would mean. I'd been alone for more than two years and I was enjoying it. I didn't want to make a decision I would be sorry for; I had done that too many times. "I need to think about this, I need time. I will let you know as soon as I know." He walked me to the door and kissed me good-bye.

Would this be the end of being alone or the continuing of life by myself?

Chapter Fifteen

T his was a big decision to make. It could be for the rest of my life. Was I ready to give up the hope of love, to live a loveless life? Maybe I would learn to love Lee. Would I be doing it for the right reason or would I be doing it only out of selfishness? Would I be able to fulfill what he wanted from me? There were so many questions, but so little answers. I started to write, making a list that Linda liked so much. The good and the bad, the right verses the wrong of it all.

The bad or wrong list consisted of whether or not I could ever love Lee. Then there was the thought of being tied down, no more freedom to come and go as I wished. Could I handle having to take care of someone else, since I couldn't always take care of myself? Giving up my home with no real guarantees that I would stay married, the pain of yet another divorce, answering to someone else and he was older than me by a decade. These questions terrified me.

On the plus side my bills would be paid, along with a home I could really call my own. Finally, I'd belong to a family. Lee and I enjoyed each other's company, and respected each other, flaws and all. It could be fulfilling to help him enjoy life more. He wasn't bad looking even if he was older. We seemed to like the same food and he enjoyed eating out and that enabled me to go places where I would not normally go. He understood that I didn't love him.

Scrutinizing at both lists, I felt I was reaching for the good. What did that mean? Was I making this harder than it was? After four failed marriages, thinking each was right for me and feeling real love was involved, they always turned out the same. Maybe not being in love was the biggest bonus. I felt that I could trust him and believe him so why was I questioning him? Would we both get more out of a marriage than we would give up? Before making my decision, I wanted to wait a few days to try the idea on.

When I called him and told him my answer was yes; he asked how soon I could move in. We set September 17th as a wedding date and I would move in right after that. He wanted to take me right then to go pick out a ring and have dinner to celebrate, Friday would have to do so plans were made.

On Friday we picked out a nice wedding set for me, but he said he didn't want a band, that was fine with me. We went out to a nice restaurant and had a good dinner and a few drinks. He said he wanted me to spend the night with him, I knew he would. I hoped I was ready and prayed I would be able to relax.

His house was plain due to his blindness, but it was clean. We sat down with beers and discussed wedding and honeymoon details. Practicality won out and we would go to the justice of peace and have no honeymoon; instead I would take time off to move in. Then he started to kiss me; it still felt like I was kissing my father. We then moved to his bedroom and took off our clothes, really kind of dry and unfeeling. We climbed into bed and faced each other. More kissing and he started to move his hands over my breast, it was ok, and I tensed a little, but felt I could deal with this. Then to my lower part and rubbing me, I in turned did the same, just like I was taught to do. I didn't feel anything, no love, no hate, nothing. He was making sounds, I was quiet. I could tell he was enjoying himself, when he was done he moved away from me saying, that was good and wanted to know if I enjoyed it. Lying, I replied that I did. He said that we would have to find ways that would make me feel more enjoyment. Although I didn't feel that was possible. Thinking logically, it seemed that once or twice a week for a man his age would probably be something I could tolerate. So we got married.

After the wedding I started to move into his, now our house. He had much older furniture than I did; he agreed that since I had the newer furnishings he would give his away. The dog liked the new house and really enjoyed having somebody there when I was at work. I wanted to decorate the house so that I too was reflected in the home. Well I was able to paint it as long as I didn't paint it pink. I told him it was not pink but light brown. Then as I was painting it I said, "This is supposed to be a light brown, but on the wall it looked pink." He told me I would have to paint it again. "Why, you won't see it." I started to laugh and told him I was just teasing him. My furniture fit well and was able to be set to the same layout; this was good because it would make it easy for Lee to maneuver. I was glad just to have my things there.

Things were working out for the most part, even though I couldn't sit items out without worry of brakeage, but there were places in the house I could make my own and that helped a lot. It was a three bedroom house so two of the bedrooms would be mine to do whatever I wanted. I made one into a craft room and the other was like my own personal room. We did share the master bedroom for sleeping.

It turned out to be quite enjoyable having someone home when I returned from work. We would sit at the kitchen table and talk about my work. Often dinner was made by Judy, which was nice too. His daughter would also do some cleaning, that helped too. I said she didn't need to worry about my two rooms; I would take care of them. The set up in the kitchen wasn't right for me, so we worked together to change some things around to make it better for me and still be easy for him to find things.

All in all things were working out between us, and we were beginning to set a way of life. We would eat out a few times a week; go to the casino from time to time, which was something Lee seemed to enjoy. Two nights a month were reserved for my friends to go "Ladies Night Out." Since I didn't always enjoyed what he wanted to watch I would go to my room to watch what I wanted or to write. I would spend time on my off days working on some craft project. I was still able to manage the nights we had sex, the kissing had all but stopped. I also found out that his biggest need during sex was that he enjoyed it. I would try to tell him when something didn't feel good or did feel good, but he would just keep doing what he liked. Unfortunately, since I wasn't enjoying it anyway, I just accepted it. He seemed to except that I would never be a wild lover. So life went on.

Chapter Sixteen

It was nice to see my bill become smaller and smaller and still have money left over to spend if I wanted to. I enjoyed making Lee special dinners on one of my days off, even if he insisted that I shouldn't spend my time off cooking. We would find that there was some subject that we couldn't agree on; mostly we would just avoided talking about them. When we didn't agreed on finances I would usually just finally agree with him, he did know more than me. He was fulfilling his part of our agreement.

Our biggest disagreement was the fact that he seemed to be supporting his daughter, financially. When she helped him out, I could understand that he wanted to give her money for that. However, it went far beyond that. He paid her rent, bought her food and clothing, paid for her two boys schooling, and gave them spending money. Although she was married, her husband didn't have a job either. Clearly they were taking advantage of Lee. Lee was a smoker and frequently would find some of them missing. When he confronted his daughter, she always denied taking them.

I was also find things missing in my craft room, and it seemed that my bedroom was being gone through, like someone was looking for something, Lee insisted I was wrong, which led me to lock my rooms. Lee said he really didn't like it but if it made me feel better it would be alright.

Lee had a very good income; he was receiving money from his disability, air force retirement, social security, and civil service retirement. He had no problem on spending money on things we needed, which really wasn't much, paying our bills, a hefty morgue payment, and buying our food. Most everything I needed and maybe half the food I would purchase. At the end of each month he was out of money, he said he wanted to pay more on the morgue but there wasn't enough. I reminded him he was supporting his daughter and her family. What was going to happen if he could no longer paid all her bills, what if he died? He would say that would then be her problem. That was the end of it. Well it was his money so I would accept that.

As with all marriages we had our problems and it seemed we both could accept them. We were still getting along very well. He was giving me my freedom and accepted that I had my own set of friends that I wanted to spend time with. Many times I would have a friend and husband over for drinks and maybe dinner, not often, but Lee seemed to enjoy it and liked my friends. We would have Nancy and Rick, Nancy's boyfriend, over too.

My bills were getting paid off, we got along and I felt I had made the right decision to marry Lee. I was still working twelve to sixteen hours a day, which made it hard to get enough sleep. Trying to work and take care of Lee was really like working two jobs at the same time. Lee and I talked about it and decided that I would step down and work less hours, have less responsibility, and less pay. It seemed it was another good decision. It also meant that I would be home more and we needed his daughter less, although it didn't change the amount of money he gave her.

Since I was getting more sleep and had more time at home I wanted to start really cleaning which I didn't do when I moved in, Lee told me his daughter always cleaned real good. Well she didn't clean she just covered up. So I cleaned up.

When he was sighted, Lee read all the time. I purchased a tape player for him and encouraged him to learn to use it so he could listen to books on tape. He said he wouldn't be able to maneuver the tape player. I tried to show him how easy it could be with just putting something on the right buttons and to make sure all tapes were put in order. He told me it sounded like a good idea and that it was great of me to think of it but, he didn't think he would be able to do it. That hurt my feelings; I really thought he would give it a try. "That's alright, I would listen to them," I said while trying not to show the hurt.

To my surprise and delight when I came home from work the next day Lee told me he had learned to work the player and that his daughter put Velcro on the buttons so he knew which was play and rewind. And that all tapes were put in the boxes in order with side one facing front. He also said that he was enjoying the first book he was listening to. I told him I was happy and that we could get more books for him. He would get to the point where he would go through two books a week.

I would make more dinners for him and always made sure there were some leftovers for his lunch the next day. His daughter was now only coming over two or three times a week now. In some ways it made it easier for me even if it meant more work.

I had gotten my car paid off and Lee kept telling me I would need to now get a new one. "Why, I like the one I have now and it was good on gas?" He would say that I could get one that was bigger and more comfortable to travel in. "Were we going to be traveling?" I asked. He said that not right away but someday when I wasn't working. Well I still had lots of time before then; I really did like my car. But, I said we could look, we did and he seemed to be picking out just the same car I had just a little bigger, not much. I felt that why trade one small car for another one? He told me that a small car would be better on gas and cost less. If I was going to trade my car it was going to be for something better, sure it would cost more but I could use my car as a trade-in. He said that he thought he would give my car to his daughter and wouldn't have a trade-in. NO, NO, NO I wasn't buying it. I just said I wanted to keep my car; it was good and gave good gas mileage. When I retired then we could look at getting a different car. If he wanted her to have a car she could just buy one for herself, or he could buy it for her. He did, and that was the end of that. Like I said there were a few things we couldn't come together on, but not many.

Every Fourth of July we would visit his family for the reunion, it was always fun and I was starting to really getting to know them, and them me. It was always a good get away and a time we didn't have to worry about other people.

Three years had gone by and Lee's health was deteriorating more. I thought he wasn't telling us everything, but most the time I was working when he went to the doctor, his daughter would take him. She never said anything, she would just wait for him never seeing or talking to the doctor. We were still having sex maybe two times a week sometimes only once, and I could tell it was harder on him now. He would always say it was fine and that the doc never told him to stop.

Well we should have, one night he wanted to have sex, I tried to put him off but he said he already took his pill and it would be a waste of twenty dollars, so I agreed. We were only in bed for maybe five minutes when he said something was wrong. All of a sudden he rolled over and started shaking, gasping for air, and his body was so tight. I tried to get him on his back and find out what was wrong. He just laid there; I jumped up and called 911. I told them what was happening and that he was just lying there now. They explained how to pump his heart and give him mouth-to-mouth, which I had learned many years before. Within five minutes there were fireman and police all over my house. There I was naked; the dog was going crazy not knowing what was going on. I threw on a robe; put the dog into the bath before letting them in. They moved Lee to the living room, where there was room to work on him. A policeman kept me in the bedroom and asked me questions. Then another policeman came in and said they were taking Lee to the hospital but he didn't think there was much hope of reviving him. He wanted to know if I could find someone to take me to the hospital; he could see I was in no condition to drive myself. I said I could call Lee's son, but when I tried I couldn't dial the number, so the policeman did. He got a hold of Lee Jr. told him what had happened and that I needed a ride to the hospital. He was over to the house within five minutes. The police helped lock the house and made sure I had my purse and keys before he and we left for the hospital. Lee Jr. said his wife was calling the other kids and they would all come to the hospital.

Lee was pronounced dead. Lee's children and grandchildren were devastated and I was stunned and shaking. Everyone kept asking me what had happened. To say that Lee had put me on the spot was an understatement.

The following week was really hard, I didn't love Lee but I thought a lot of him and knew I would miss him. I thought we would have longer together. A couple of my kids came to stay with me for a while and support me. I was glad of that. I talked to the family in his hometown; several would be coming to the funeral. They were all so supportive of me, which helped very much. As for his children, it was a different story, a couple seemed to blame me; I should have known that he was having trouble. I would try to explain that I was always unable to take him to the doctor's but his daughter did. Whatever was wrong, Lee shared with no one. He lived his life the way he wanted; and died the way he wanted.

There were some items that Lee had, and he had me make a list of them and who was to get them, he then say everything else would belong to me. Lucky he had money for the funeral, but his kids weren't agreeing on how it should be, finally it was decided on. On the day Lee was buried I had asked everybody to come to my house because there were some things that Lee wanted them to have.

I read Lee's list that I had written for him and distributed everything accordingly. His children were not happy and argued about what they wanted. As they were tearing through my house, my children and Lee's family intervened and sent his children away. Lee's brother and niece said his children had gotten all they were supposed to and if they caused any more trouble, they would take care of it. Yes, he had a good family; it was his kids who were wrong. Now I was on my own again, but better off.

Finding What I Lost

You cannot know what you have never had.

But, you can know a loss of love without ever being loved.

Knowing love leaves you open for hurt.

Yet, you can hurt if you are never loved.

You don't have a life if you are not loved.

Then again, without love you can live.

One moment of love can give enough happiness and life to
live until the end.

Chapter Seventeen

Eventually all the legal work was finished and I didn't end up doing too badly. Although the house still had a mortgage, I was able to receive some of Lee's disability, which I didn't expect; I should be able to make monthly payments. Also, upon my own retirement, I would get Lee's social security. Aside from already going to the altar five times, that was another good reason to stay single. I even thought I would be happier if I never had another boyfriend.

I cared and respected Lee, I will miss him but now it is time to make this house my home. It would probably take years to get it there. Lee died in October, so now it would mean that I would be going through the holidays alone again. My children felt it should be different, three of them and five grandchildren came to spend Christmas with me. I also found out that one would be moving here, in about three months, which will be nice. I was kept busy until the day after Christmas, and then all was quiet again. I still had my dog but she was going blind, not much could be done and she was very healthy. I hated leaving her alone so I got another dog. This time it was a male, he would be the man of the house.

After the holidays, thing began to get back to normal, or what would become my normal. I was driving home on Friday and saw a little bar only two blocks from my home so I stopped in for a beer. There I meet a nice lady and her friend, we seemed to get along. The one named Toni told me it was a nice and friendly place and they were regulars and said I should come back. In fact, the next afternoon I did go back and Toni, my new friend, was there. We had a few beers and found that we had art in common. She was maybe ten years younger than me and a bit on the quiet side, so I did a lot of talking. It was nice to have someone to talk to now that I was alone again. This became a habit a few times a week, to stop in have a drink and chat with Toni.

One day when I stopped by to see Toni, she had a friend with her. She introduced us; his name was Steve. I was taken by him at once. He was just a little older than me, about five nine or better, he had the most compelling eyes, and a fabulous smile. He was clean cut, with slacks and a nice buttoned up shirt. His demeanor was that of a company president. He said he was in real estate. Steve was generous and bought the drink as we sat and talked.

The next time I went in they both, Toni and Steve, were there so I joined them. I found him to be quite appalling and when Toni excused herself to go to the ladies' room; Steve asked if I would go out with him. I asked if he was dating Toni, if so, I couldn't go out with him, it wouldn't be right. He said that Toni was just a friend, he couldn't think about any other way. I said that she liked him and I didn't want to invade her territory. He said I wouldn't be. When Toni came back Steve wanted to take us to this place where there was always karaoke, he wanted us to come. Toni wanted to go and wanted me to go so I did. Steve had a friend there that we sat with. The whole time we were there it seemed Steve was giving Toni more attention than 'just friends'. When I went up to the bar Steve came up behind me and asked me again to go out with him. "If she isn't your girlfriend you sure are treating her like you wanted her to be. I told you she would have to tell me it was alright." I went back to my seat.

The next day Toni and I were able to talk, I told her that Steve had asked me out and my subsequent conversation with him. She also insisted she was just his friend and that I should go out with him, I was more his age. I don't know if she was telling me what she really felt. Steve did show up and sat by me, not Toni. Again he asked me out, and Toni said I should go out with him. So on Sunday we went out for a few beers. I told him that maybe Toni did say I should go out with him but I think she really liked him. He said she was nice and was a friend that was all. He said that I was different; he said that he really wanted to get close to me, 'if I knew what he meant'. I informed him I wasn't that easy, I had to know the person before I got close, 'if he knew what I meant'. He said that was just what he wanted, and when would I go out with him again. I told him I had to get up early for work, but next Friday would be fine. That is great, but maybe we could get together before then for a drink or two, he asked for my phone number. I agreed and gave him my number. I really didn't think I would hear from him. I did, two days later.

We met for drinks, but this time we didn't talk about Toni, we talked about ourselves. He told me about his business ventures, and that he wasn't married and never would. I told him I had been married five times and nothing worked out and I never would get married again. The second date work out great and would see each other on Friday. I was looking forward to that.

The next day I stopped to see Toni again, see if she knew I had gone out with Steve. When I asked her if she had seen him she said no and said that she thought it would be fine if I was to go out with him. She also told me he was living with a lady. According to Toni, Steve and his roommate had been in a relationship many years ago, but now just shared a house. I didn't say anything more about Steve.

When Friday rolled around Steve called to make sure we were still on and where to pick me up. He took me to a really nice restaurant and we had a good dinner. I told him what Toni said and he confirmed it. He said that they were lover for ten years, but she became ill from diabetes, was losing her eyesight and her hearing and was on lots of medication. Her personality changed and she became mean and frustrated. Their relationship changed to that of two people sharing a house they had purchased together many years before, with neither one wanting to relinquish their share to the other. Eventually, Steve began making his own life, while she stayed in the house as a semi-invalid. This sounded strange but if it was true, it meant that our relationship would be very limited. Maybe that would be good for me. I did feel a draw to him, not sure why. He was very charming.

On our way to my house I knew I wouldn't have sex with him tonight. It just wasn't right. When we got to my house I asked him in for a drink. We sat on the couch and before long we were kissing, he then made a move towards my breast. I told him that even though I was attracted to him it was just a little too soon. He did seem to accept that without being upset. He said we could go out again tomorrow night if I wanted to.

After he left I took time to think about what I was doing and how I felt about it. I wasn't sure why I felt differently about him, but I knew I did. The thing was that when he reached for my breast and touched them I didn't tense up. Why didn't that bother me, usually it did. I still didn't know why I was drawn to him but it might be worth it to find out. Tomorrow night we would see.

Dinner was great; he seemed to know all the right places to go. He always provided good conversation; with interesting topics and never too much. His listening skills were just as good. All the way home I had only one thought on my mind and knew he did too.

When we got to my house, he went around opening my door to let me out. It seemed I was in his arms even before I realized it. His lips on mine, kissing me like I was the only woman in the world. He wanted to enjoy every moment of it and the feel of me. In his kisses I relived every happy moment I ever had. By the time we made it inside the house my body was telling me to go for it. I was ready to finally give myself to a man, no holding back, no tensing up.

He was sitting on the couch with my two dogs; I slipped away to my bedroom. I really wanted this night to be right, to be something I had never known, something special. Placing candles around gave a low romantic light. The bed was made and the room looked like a love bungalow. I took him by the hands, hoping he couldn't feel the trembling in my own, and then we were there. He was sitting on the bed holding me, kissing me; I was getting lost in them. He was kissing my neck then down my blouse. So sweet, loving and soft; I couldn't believe he could make me feel that way. I feared removing my clothes; my body wasn't what it had been at one time. He told me I was beautiful and I felt beautiful.

To have a man's hand caress my breast and not tense up was like magic. The way he looked at them and kissed them sent sparks of heat running throughout my whole body. Playing with each, making them rise to his touch. Feeling a longing I had never felt, it was wielding up from my womanhood to my fingers tips, to the top of my head. I wanted him like I never wanted anyone before. I unbuttoned his shirt and glad to see he too was imperfect and it didn't bother him at all.

When I finally had his pants off and mine lay beside his he pulled me onto the bed never once losing contact with my body. As his hands moved down my body he hit a very ticklish spot, I couldn't help but laugh. "Ticklish are you?" He said with a laugh in his voice and a devilish look in his eyes. I couldn't help but laugh again and he laughed with me. He started to move his hand down my body making sure he didn't hit the same spot, leaving heat and desire everywhere he touched. I began doing the same, but not like I was taught, but letting my feelings guide me. He had a full chest of hair, it was ever so soft; and his nipples were as hard as mine. When I reached his belly, it felt natural under my hand. Finally caressing his well-endowed manhood; "Oh, my God how could I manage this, is this going to work?" I didn't mean to say that out loud but I must have, he laughed "Don't worry baby, I will take care of you, no hurting." He laughed again so did I. It did feel so good in my hand and I could feel the heat rising in him.

He was adding his heat to my body knowing just where to touch, to rub, to roll between his fingers. I can't remember any man I was ever with that had such knowledge of the female body. My insides seemed to be calling out for him. He stopped kissing me and started moving his mouth down my body, I wanted to stop him, and I knew where he was going and feared it would mess everything up. I very rarely would let a man do this to me and when I did it never turned out good. But I couldn't stop him it felt so good so right,

Then I felt his tongue touch me and he was working every part of my body in a way it had never been and making me ache for more. My hand on top of his head helping his movements, I felt like I was going to explode, and then I did. My body was vibrating, my head was spinning and a feeling of completeness covered me. He knew what was happening and he went with it never letting up until it was over.

Then he moved up beside me and reaches for a drink of his beer, "WHOO! That was fabulous! He planted a big kiss on me. I can't remember being kissed so much and so lovingly. Then he moved his body on top of mine, slowly, smoothly like he was afraid he would hurt me. He didn't. I opened myself for him; I wanted him inside of me. I wanted all of him and he was more than happy to give it to me. Asking if he was hurting me, he was but it felt too good to stop. Then it happened again and it was as good as the first one. We were both spent and could hardly move.

He rolled off me and took me in his arms, "I have never had a woman like you." He kissed me and took me even tighter in his arms and we fell asleep.

We woke up a little later. He said he had to leave as much as he didn't want to, he got dressed and I put on my robe. I walked him to the door where he kissed me one more time, "I'll call you tomorrow." And he left.

This was to be the beginning of many nights and days together.

Chapter Eighteen

The next day I woke up with a smile on my face, I can't remember ever doing that. I didn't understand why last night made me feel the way I felt. For the first time being with a man brought no thoughts of my past, no fear, or disgust for what was being done to me. These feelings of wonder and caring were foreign to me. Strange, it took all these years and one man to show me what it meant to make love, to care about the other. Now for the first time I understood what women were talking about. Just to think about it now was making me want him; could it be I have also learned to desire someone? What has this man done to me? Is this the way it will always be, is it only him I can feel this way with? So many questions and no answers, but this time I didn't care about answers. I will accept it as a gift.

He texted me in the morning and said he would be over around two that afternoon. I was anxious to see him. I wanted to know how he felt about last night and I wanted to know if I would see him as the same person. Of course I immediately cleaned the room changed the bed sheets and replaced the candles with new ones. I showered and dressed and even put on eye make-up. I looked at myself in the mirror and saw an old lady looking back. This was crazy I was acting like a teenager; I was feeling like a teenager. A thought pasted my mind. Would it have been that way with Bill? I had hoped so.

When two o'clock came and went, I worried that he might not show. He was half an hour late, which soon became apparent that he was frequently late. He was going to take me to some of his hangouts. It was fun; he knew so many places and people. He proudly introduced me to all of them. We stopped at one placed and had dinner. It was a fun day; he was so attentive towards me. He would hold my hand, put his arm around me but kisses only when we were in the car alone. After dinner we stopped at one more place, before heading home. Heading home I could feel myself become amorous and anxious at the same time. My feelings were taking control of me and I wasn't sure that I liked it.

Once we were in the house, my questions were answered. We were all over each other, kissing, hugging and touching, so we moved to the bedroom. I started the candles. We had fun undressing each other. We would laugh after each piece of clothing came off; I still didn't know what was so funny. We climbed into bed and our lovemaking started much the same as the night before. This time there was more talking, what felt good, what wasn't good. Even though I'd been married many times, I said I was a prude and hadn't enjoyed sex in the past; that I only did it as a chore. He assured me that I had left him well satisfied. While he insisted that he had forgotten any woman he had been with before, I had to laugh to myself, thinking it couldn't be possible. I just said thank you and got back to what we were doing. We fell asleep in each other's arms to wake up about an hour later. He got dress and kissed me good-bye saying he would call me. I slept very well that night.

Was this really happening to me? Given my prior experiences, it was hard to grasp, let alone believe it. True to his world of the night before, he called the next morning to invite me to breakfast. He picked me up and we went to a nearby restaurant then went back to my house. Deciding to get profound, I asked him what our relationship meant to him. "It means that we have had a good time together and hopeful more in the future. What does it mean to you?"

Wanting to be truthful I said, "I'd like to say we are seeing each other exclusively." When I saw the concern on his face, I stopped talking. Was I scaring him away? Then I said, "That's what I would have said four years ago. Now my answer is that I don't want to get married again, I don't want to be tied down, I enjoy my freedom."

He looked me in the eye, "That is how I feel; I do see other women and probable will continue to do so." He grabbed my hand "What do you really want?" He asked.

"I do want to see you again, I enjoy spending time with you and I want to make love to you and would hope we can do it again and again. My feeling is when you are involved with someone and enjoy making love with that person; you shouldn't need to make love with others."

He said he understood and he would think about it. He almost looked like I was challenging him. I was just telling him how I felt, and I think I was a little hurt. "Just do me a favor, if you find someone you want to sleep with, at least tell me, so we can just become friends?" He said he would. We talked a bit more, and then he left.

Now I was confused, I had never been with a man like we had been; and didn't become a pair. I didn't know what to do. I meant it, I didn't and still don't want to get married, or even tied down; but after being with Steve and the way he made me feel, I couldn't see myself being with anyone else. If what he had said to me about the way I made him feel how he could even think about being with someone else. This is all new to me. Is this the way things are these days, or was he just giving me 'a line'?

He texted me the next day to say he would be in his office all day. He wanted to know what I had planned beside work. I told him I had several things I had to do at home after work. He texted back saying he had a nice time yesterday and he was still thinking about our weekend together; he would call me tomorrow. This was good I needed to spend time by myself.

On the way home I stop to talk to Toni, I felt I needed to tell her that Steve and I had been seeing a lot of each other. She was there at the bar as she always was, I think she lived there. We took a corner table and I told her about the last few days with Steve. She became irate, accusing me of stealing him from her. I reminded her that she was the one who told me to go out with him in the first place. She wouldn't hear any of it, not wanting to argue with her, I left. It appeared that I lost a friend over this man, but this was more than a man to me. Maybe later she would see things differently.

For the next two weeks Steve and I would see each other three or four times a week and Steve would stay late twice a week. I enjoyed that time; I enjoyed being with him and making love with him. I still didn't quite understand him but I was ready to accept him the way he was. At least that is what I told myself.

On the third week after our great night I didn't see him. He would text me most every day asking how I was but he was always too busy to see me. Was it over? Had he already found someone else? So I guess that was that. I thought he had cared for me. It was so painful, I really missed him. Now Toni wouldn't have to be mad, I was in her shoes.

Chapter Nineteen

On the second Friday of not seeing him he text saying he would like to see me later. After thinking about, I did want to see him even if it was to find out what was wrong. I felt I had done something wrong. I text him back "OK, what time?"

He was almost on time, and he still looked as cute as ever. He planted a big kiss on me and said he had missed me. He still made me feel special. I asked if I'd done something wrong. "NO, you couldn't do anything wrong. I have just been so busy." He kissed me again.

He sat down on the couch and played with the dogs a bit. Asked me where I felt like eating? I didn't really know many places, "I don't care, what do you feel like having?" He said steaks and he knew a good place for them. I said that sounds good. He really did know the best places to go.

After dinner, which was good, we found a nice little bar that was just about four blocks from my house so we tried it out. It seemed nice, clean and quiet. We had a drink then headed for home. The loving was as good as it was before. Finally, we fell asleep as always. This time I didn't wake up when he left.

Next day, he text me to meet him at a restaurant where he was having breakfast with friends he would like me to meet. I didn't understand him; we spent almost two weeks apart, now he wants to see me for the second day in a row. I was so confused, but was glad to meet him. Again he was proud to introduce me, I never felt cheap around him. We went to the show afterwards. Then we each went to our respective homes.

The next day we met for drinks and talk for about two hours. We parted, which was good I had washing to do. I had told him I would be retiring next week and it would be nice to see him. He said I would.

It was a busy week for me, finishing things up at work, seeing Steve a few times, and planning a retiring party. The party was on Friday night and I saw several friends there, it was a good time. It was a better after party just Steve and I. He was always good.

It looked like we were back to seeing each other, I just don't know how I am supposed to act or feel. I want to be with him, maybe more than he wanted to be with me. Was he just using me for sex? I didn't feel that was his only reason for being with me. Was I expected just to ignore him seeing other ladies when he wasn't seeing me? Suddenly, I felt like I was moving backwards.

When I tried to pin him down on his feeling he would say "Be cool, everything is fine." What did that mean? I think the question I need to ask is what I needed out of this relationship, where did I want it to go. I was feeling like my "old" self and that was destructive. I knew I wanted more from him, I didn't want to get married, I still don't want anyone to move in with me, I wanted my freedom. This sounds like a contradiction. This whole thing was feeling unhealthy for me. Yet I wasn't ready to give him up.

He did call and asked if I would have dinner with him, I said yes but, why don't we eat in. I said I wasn't the best cook but I could make good spaghetti. He seemed to like that idea. We set a time, of course he was late. He said he had stop in to see Toni before coming. I asked how she was and if she knew that he was coming to my house? He said she was the same, she was still spending all her time at the bar, and her car broke down. He gave her some money. And yes, he told her he was headed to my house for dinner.

He said the dinner was great and he ate too much. We watched a movie and then he went home. If it wasn't for all the kissing I would think we were nothing but good old buddies. But, it was nice to see him. We didn't see each other the next day just got a text.

The need to get my mind on something else was strong. I decided to start fixing the house; I would start with my bed room. This actually helped keep my mind off Steve. I wouldn't see him again for three days and he wasn't answering all my texts. Luckily, it didn't seem to bother me.

When he called he wanted to take me to one of his houses to get my opinion on some things. "This was different, what the heck?" It was a house he was thinking of moving his office into and away from home. It still had some work to finish it but he wanted to know how to decorate it. He seemed to like all my ideas, and asked if I would do it for him, he would pay me. The money would come in handy since I was doing my house too. So now I was one of his employees. What did this mean? We went out for dinner and he stayed late that night.

I felt like I was on a roller-coaster, with very high ups and very low downs. My desire to be with him all the time was strong. The need to be a big part of his life; waiting around for him to call, changing any plans just to be with him, where was that freedom I was telling myself I wanted? I knew I needed to let go, but I couldn't even if I wanted to. Was I just lying to myself, did I really want to change? Was my desire for him love or lust? I have to let go.

Chapter Twenty

When Lee was alive, we had to keep the house simple and free from clutter so he could get around freely. I hadn't unpacked everything I had brought to his house. Now, as I started to unpack all the items I found I still had so much. Apparently, I didn't get rid of as much as I thought. This went way beyond Aunt Billie's craft basket; I now have enough craft items for three rooms. I have enough books for a small library. I have saved pictures, gifts from kids, and clothes. I even have five televisions and five dressers. What a pack rat I'd been. I will have to get rid of so much, hope I can do it.

Six years ago I started to rid myself of emotional baggage, but I know that I am still hanging on to some; Steve has showed me that. But, now was the time to clean out the physical baggage of my life. I see this will be a huge project. Trying to get rid of old memories, I find that I was hanging onto items that have all the memories buried deep inside of them. I pick up an item that David had given me; my mind is flooded with them and him. My hand felt like it was burning just holding it. Why do we hang onto things? I see that I need to not just work on my mind but also my life. I need to get rid of the old ways of thinking and the old ways of living.

It is time to put the past in the past. I am glad I have the whole day to work on this; tomorrow I head to Steve's office house to start my new job.

I woke up around six in the morning, feeling I could use about five more hours, I worked until three in the morning. Well worth every hour, I got a lot accomplished. Steve called about eight and wanted to meet at the office house. There were three small bedrooms, living room-dinning combo and a small kitchen, also two bathrooms. With pen and paper in hand we went from room to room, jotting down notes for each. We headed for the nearest Lowe's store. There we looked at the wallpaper books; he went for some big murals. We ordered one for each bedroom which will be offices. Paint for the rooms and odds and ends that are missing and needs to be fixed. From the store we went to lunch, and discussed ideas for the new office. He liked everything I was coming up with. He said, "Anything you think, I know you will make it great." He wanted to know when I was going to start. Since today is more than half over we scheduled to begin work the next day. He was even supplying one of his construction workers to help me out with whatever I need.

After lunch I went home and moved all my bags of items to the back porch. I moved all the furniture out of the bedroom. Now that it was empty I started planning the makeover for my room. It was an early night.

The next day at the office house I had a surprise visitor, Steve's secretary. Steve sent her out to pick the room she wanted for her office. I found that she had been working for Steve for fifteen years. She was an interesting lady, and I liked her. She had known that Steve and I had been dating for a while and said she liked me better than any of his other girlfriends. This was also an opportunity to find out more about Steve. She did confirm what he had said about his roommate. In fact, that was the main reason for moving the offices out of his house. It was difficult to get much work done at the house with his roommate always interrupting to ask about Steve's business or needing some assistance with her own problems. I think I found a real person that I could talk to, someone that had a brain on her head. Steve's man showed up and I walked with him and showed him what needed to change or get finished. He wasn't well educated, and had some troubles with the law, but he seemed nice enough and a hard worker. Steve seemed to have a need to be with and help this type of person. I spent the rest of the day painting. Steve stopped by and took me to lunch. He has planned to go shopping for some furniture later that week and wanted me to go with him. He also wanted to meet for drinks after work, we made the plans.

In my earlier years I pretty much kept my mouth shut except those times I had to mouth off. As I've gotten older, I seem to talk nonstop. Steve would laugh and say my mind was a treadmill, it just kept running; he was amazed at how much I knew. "You are amazing," getting that sweet smile on his face that I enjoy seeing.

For the next few weeks, life settled in to a routine. I would work on office three days a week. In my free time I'd work on my own house. Then I'd go with Steve to any sale he found. He would stay late once or twice a week. On one night he told me that his roommate would be gone for a week visiting her family. He wanted me to spend the week with him at his house. "You mean that we would go to bed with each other at night and wake-up with each other in the morning?" He said yes, he would really like that. Of course, my answer was yes.

It will be interesting to see where he spends his time at night; and maybe how he spends his time each day. I was looking forward to next week. I didn't hear from him the rest of the week. The thought that popped into my head was that he was seeing other women; the thought was still hard to think about. I was able to console myself with the thought that it was me he asked to stay with him.

Each time we were together I would learn a little more about him. Now I hope that some questions would be answered. One important thing I learned is that Steve would always call even if it was a week later. I would always be waiting for that call, and go running to him. This still bothered me that I felt that way.

Chapter Twenty-one

I am really looking forward to having a whole week with Steve, but I have my own concerns. Being with him for six days twenty-four hours a day may be too much of him for me or me for him. I am to meet him at a shopping center close to his home in about two hours. My next door neighbor will be caring for my dogs. In a way I feel like this is our first date, I wonder how it will go. It has been a year since I have had any one sleeping with me and I know that I don't sleep well so I hope we don't brother each other. Well here goes.

I was glad; for once he was on time. I knew he lived on a hill but didn't realize that it overlooked so much of the city. The house itself is twice the size of my own. It has all high end finishes and lots of room. It had only three bedrooms which left lots of space for the kitchen, living, dinning and family rooms. I thought that my house was full of stuff; my oh my he has stuff. It has big windows so there is lots of light which I really like as long as it is private. This house is so private that you could run around naked and no one would see you. Now I am not big on cooking but I could really enjoy cooking in this kitchen. The big screen TV will be nice to watch, I might even be able to read the writing on it. As for his bedroom, it is a good size larger than mine.

It has a king plus size bed and its own bathroom. Well, in a bed that big maybe my moving around won't bother him too much. There is a large sliding glass door that opens onto a covered patio extending the length of the house in the back. There is a sparkling swimming pool, ever so inviting, with a Ramada. Like being on vacation!

It has been almost a week since we last saw each other but every time I see him it is like I just left him. He never changes, and even though he doesn't see me he keeps up on me. He is really enjoying showing me around the house, his pride and joys, pictures, and on and on. I think it took over two hours just to see everything he wanted me to see.

We ran out for a quick dinner, there is nothing quick about Steve, so it was well after ten by the time we got back. It had been a warm day and I wanted to get into that pool so bad so when we got back we jumped. It was great but we didn't stay in long. We were both so tired that we hit the bed laid in each other's arms and fell asleep. I woke up about four to find him already up. He was just getting ready to get back into bed; I was ready to get up. I stayed in bed long enough for him to fall asleep. I slipped out to watch my favorite early shows, then a dip in the pool. When I was ready to get out of the pool he was getting up.

We sat and had coffee and there were three calls he had too answer already. He then fixed himself something to eat. As for me, I need to be up five or six hours before I eat. Steve said that would change because he loved going out for breakfast and the few times we did I didn't eat enough. So now he is a health nut. I explain to him that my eating habits were tied to my mental outlook. I wasn't much on eating, in fact there were days that when I am busy I forget to eat. He thought I was all wrong but he wasn't the first that thought that. Another cup of coffee was all I needed. Before he was done eating he had four more calls, his workers checking in. Then his secretary show up. She didn't seem surprised to see me there at all. We greeted each other and talked for a bit then she went to work. He said he had some work to do so I would have the run of the house, make myself at home.

Later he had some errands to run so he took me with him. While out we got lunch, and did some shopping for food. I told him I would make dinner. After the errands then a stop at what I call 'my pub' and checking on dogs we were home by six. I started the pork chops and then we jumped in the pool. We both finished making dinner, and enjoyed it. I told him I wasn't much of a cook, he just laughed. That comment would come back on me many times.

Turning on the television, we found our different likes and dislikes. His favorites are the news and old westerns, mine are science fiction movies. As long as I was sitting wrapped in his arms, it didn't matter what was on. It was nice, before long we were kissing and heading for the bedroom. The lovemaking with him is completely satisfying. For the second night in a row we fell asleep in each other's arms. I woke up about one hour later knowing it was too early to get up, he was awake about ten minutes after me. We both went to the kitchen and talked for about half an hour then headed back to bed and went back to sleep.

It must have been about six-thirty when I woke up, which was late for me. I started to get out of bed when a hand grabbed me. "Where are you going?" He told me not to move and went to the bathroom. Five minutes later he was back, now it was my turn. When I got back in bed he was all over me. He began kissing me from head to toe. He was like a wild man there wasn't an inch of my body that he didn't touch, didn't kiss. The love making was wild and very intense. "This is what I feel like doing many mornings after we had been together the night before," he said.

When I wake up to him like this it is like being the real us; wild and crazy.

When we finally got up and went to the kitchen I already felt like I had been up all day. I wanted to go to the office house to check on what was done and what was left, he too had things to do and he said he would come by the office house when he was done.

He showed up about two and asked if I had eaten, well, no. He wanted to take me and my helper to lunch, so I called it quits for the day. We went over what needed to happen tomorrow and agreed to be there about eight the next morning; we left for lunch. At lunch Steve ran into his old friend, he has lots of them; he invited him and his girlfriend over for the night. So after lunch we went shopping again. When we got home I started fixing food and he started cleaning up the house. I think my years of marriage and his living with someone prepared us for this kind of thing; we were acting like old married people. When his friend showed up we were ready for them. He took them on a tour of the house; then we headed for the pool. It was a nice night and we all enjoyed ourselves. When they left we were more than ready for bed. I still can't describe the feeling I have getting into bed at night with someone I really care about. I've had to spend so many nights getting into bed with someone I despised.

Our week was quickly coming to an end, but I think I learned a lot about Steve. I don't know what he has learned or how he feels about being with me so much, maybe he will say something. I Spent about five hours at the office house and went back to his home. He wasn't there. I couldn't get into the house but I could get into the back yard. My mind was going places it didn't need to go. This is the old me showing its face. Where was he, who is he with, what is he doing? I didn't like feeling that way but I was having a hard time pushing them away.

He showed up about an hour later. Yes, he had stopped to see Toni then came home to me. I think I was feeling threatened by her. But, he was home to see me. I fixed a simple dinner of left overs, he couldn't leave too much as evidence of someone else being there. I think I was feeling resentment towards his roommate too. I wasn't going to let that get in my way; we were together now so enjoy it.

After dinner we went for a swim. It was dark by the time we got into the pool, the lights of the city was a sight to see. We were swimming in the nude and when he came to me and held me in his arms and started to kiss me, I went right to heaven. The only thing that could have made it perfect was if we both had gills. We got out of the pool and just sat there watching the city sparkle.

That night our lovemaking was almost as good as the first night, if we only had the candles. Falling asleep in his arms is something I can't describe.

This being Friday he had to spend time in the office, so I took the time to run home to check the dogs and mail. Went by the office house to check in; see if they needed anything. I called Steve this time to make sure he would be home. This would be our last night, I go home tomorrow. When I got to the house he was ready to go out and party. We hit three different bars and then had dinner. When we got home he was quiet, I didn't know what was on his mind. We were watching TV when he started talking.

"I have enjoyed having you here this week, I know we have our differences but they don't seem big." This I had to agree to. "I go to my home town once a year and I want to know if you will come with me this year." He seemed excited by just asking me.

"With all the expense I have fixing the house I don't think I can afford it." The idea that he asked me was great.

"I will pay for the trip; really I would like you to come."

"Yes I would like that too." I felt like jumping for joy.

"OK, let's get the tickets right now." He was pulling me to the computer room.

That night we didn't make love but held each other like there was no tomorrow.

It is Saturday, the week went so fast, I hated to see it end; but all good things must end. I got up and took one last swim. I then scoured the house to make sure I didn't leave any signs of being there, this was a strange feeling. He never really hides his feelings towards me in public but he still didn't want his roommate to know. I loaded all my things into my car and went in to have a last morning with Steve. To me it was sad but I had our trip to look forward to. Just think three weeks.

We spent the day shopping for things to use in the office; we found some good deals and dropped them off. We went for drinks and then dinner. After dinner we parted our ways, it was a sad moment for me. My dogs were glad to have me home.

I knew I was trying to dig in and hold my place in his heart. I knew I wanted to hear him tell me he loved me. Was I setting myself up for a big hurt? In my mind I am sure I knew he would never tell me what I wanted to hear but, my feelings held fast. I was feeling disappointment with myself, like I am failing myself.

The Real Missing Piece

Longing for happiness for so long

I over looked that which has always been.

Always in the wrong places and the wrong way

It was there but to clear and easy to see.

I worked so hard to find it, thought I would die from exhaustion.

Plainly, it was too simple to find.

When I stop trying and just let it come

It jumped out at me and I saw it for what it was.

12-21-2012

Chapter Twenty-two

What a great week, but back to work and life. I still have a lot of work at Steve's office and my house. The wallpaper arrived and needs to be hung. I worked all day, expecting Steve to show up, but he never did. He didn't call either, which surprised me. What could have happened now? Tomorrow I will stay home and work there.

Today I will lay the tile on my bedroom floor, and Steve still hasn't called. I don't know how many times I checked my phone to see if there was a call I missed, but not one. I worried about it all day, thinking I'd done something wrong. Although there was plenty of work at my house to keep me busy, I still kept thinking about him. This is crazy; I'm acting like a wife that was a scary thought. It is time for bed and still no word, nor answer to my text. Well, no sense in chasing him, at least that's what I told myself.

Back to Steve's house maybe I will see him. Most of the paper is up, just one room left. Finally, received a text from Steve saying he was very busy, see me later. That was all I heard for the day. This is crazy, something must be wrong with my convictions.

Staying home again, checking my phone every half hour. This can't be right, the way I am acting. Even though I told myself I wouldn't let it affect me if he'd found someone else, I couldn't convince myself. I am trying but I keep looking at the phone. I guess it is time to write.

Normal, what is that? Is there such a thing? What's normal for one person may not be normal for another person. I write two pages on this subject and still didn't find an answer. Who can I ask? Maybe I am asking the wrong questions. Not hearing from Steve left me very unhappy. I didn't do anything wrong, it doesn't have anything to do with me. Obviously, my ideas and his are not on the same page. What is "normal" for me is not "normal" for him. Could he really care for anybody but himself?

The whole situation takes me back to the beginning. Maybe I am asking the wrong questions, I keep writing. Now I ask what "I" am doing not Steve. I am trying to define my worth through what Steve says about me. It is so easy to take steps backwards without even knowing it. Trying to be honest with myself is hard. What do I want from Steve? I want him to love me, I want him to always be with me, and I want him to make me happy. That's how I ended up marrying and divorcing four times. I don't want to go back to the beginning. What have I learned? There is only one person who can make me believe I am worthy, it is me.

Maybe people like me need to tell ourselves more often how great we are, we need to give ourselves a pat on the back. Maybe even those who didn't go through what I did have to do the same sometimes. But, what about Steve, what will I do? Either I can accept what we do have and let him be him. Or, I just quit seeing him altogether. Being brave and saying

I'll stop seeing him is easier said than done. As soon as he calls, I know I will meet him. I guess that I will have to accept him and who he is.

Well it is Friday, I am not going to sit at home tonight, and if Steve doesn't call I will go out, maybe see other friends and have a good time. There is a text; Steve wants to meet for lunch, and of course, I say yes.

It seems that no matter how mad or upset I am when he walks up and smiles at me, all is forgotten. Did I waste a day, we will see. Actually it is payday and he has my check, I had forgotten that. After lunch he wants me to ride with him to do some chores. In the car we engage in light chatter. Quite honestly, I'm afraid to ask where he has been and why hasn't he called me? We past the day away and he drops me off at my car, he plans on following me home.

Once inside, he sits on the couch and plays with the dogs, he really likes them and they like him too. I bring in the beer and hand him one and turn to sit in the chair. He takes my hand and pats the couch next to him, "Sit here by me." He puts his arms around me and gives me a big kiss. He tells me he can't stay long he has to go home. I couldn't understand that.

"Why did you even come over?" I guess I am going to get into it.

"I wanted to see you and hold you, I have missed you."

"Why haven't you called me all week? Are you seeing someone else?"

"I have been really busy with things I had to do at home. Yes, I have seen other women, they are friends." He looks puzzled at me. "You remember that lady I told you about earlier, the one that had the epileptic attack?"

I thought for a moment, "Yes." She was some lady that let her boyfriend beat on her and wouldn't leave him. I seem to remember he said she didn't have much and was always in need of money.

"Well it was me that saw the attack; it was me that call the hospital. We didn't do anything." I think he could see I was getting upset, I did move away from him.

"OK, I know we said we could see other people, but it would have been nice to hear from you." I wasn't upset I was hurt.

He stood up to leave, walked over to me and said, "I may see other women but you are the only one I sleep with." He kissed me and left.

Of course, I felt that I'd made a fool of myself, again. I had gotten my answers and then some. I texted him and said he was right and I was sorry but he was also wrong for not calling me for a week. He texted back with "Be cool everything is fine, see you tomorrow." Again, I try to tell myself to accept him for what he is. I'm having a difficult time convincing myself.

Chapter Twenty-three

The next month was much the same, we were seeing each other four or five times a week, spending all day Saturday together, he would stay late two times a week. He hadn't changed; he often didn't answer my texts, show up on time, or see me when he said he would. It's becoming a way of life, waiting for him and guessing if he'll answer or not, come around or not. Unfortunately, the jealously factor stills rears its ugly head, but I try not to let it get the best of me. Accept, accept, accept is what I keep reminding myself.

Our three-week vacation was approaching. My anticipation had been growing and I was excited to get going. Being with Steve every day, getting out of town and going to the shore, what could be better! We took a flight to his hometown and rented a car to drive to his house by the water.

When we arrived, it was nothing that I'd expected. Unlike his house that was at least twice the size of mine, sitting on a hill with land to put two more houses on; this was a small mobile home on a small lot. The one good thing was that instead of a pool, this house was ten steps from a beautiful lake. After unpacking, we drove into town to get dinner and some supplies, saw the town, which is very different than home, and headed back to his place.

The mobile consisted of two small bedrooms, each with a twin bed. No king-sized beds here, so we spent the first night in our 'own' rooms, an arrangement I had not anticipated. About three in the morning I awoke and quietly went into the living room to read my book. After ten minutes, Steve was up too. It felt strange and pleasurable to see him walk out and greet me. It would be so nice if it could last forever. He didn't stay up long and went back to bed for about another three hours. Eventually, he awoke and we had coffee, he thought it was great to have the coffee ready and waiting for him, then we discussed plans for the day. It had been a year since he was last here, so the house needed to be checked out and he had to get his boat.

We found more than we bargained for and had a lot to tackle. There were leaks in some of the rooms, the carpet in sunroom was moldy, there were spiders everywhere and cleaning was definitely needed. We would start with the sunroom by first removing the carpet. Then we discussed how to redecorate it. Steve had a handyman to help with the leaks and then we called it a day and went to get the boat and relax on the lake.

It was a very nice boat, made for speed and the moment Steve sat in the captain's seat he became a different person. He was smiling and free of worries. This was a Steve I could definitely get used to, I liked the other one but this one was more exciting and fun. Boating was great and the sights were beautiful, like being in paradise.

When we went to dinner, he was very affectionate, holding me close and kissing me in public, the captain was still there. Arriving home in throes of passion, sleeping in separate rooms was not an option. Creativity called for throwing some blankets and pillows on the floor. The romance began. He is a passionate man but that night he was more than normal. He was very personal, wanting to know the ways he could really please me more. I didn't know how he could do more but he did. We stayed on the floor until morning.

I was up first and made coffee. Our day began. His handyman, Andy, came over and checked the place. There was more damage than at first anticipated. Steve said Andy could work alone that day while he took me sightseeing. At home he would have stayed there until he knew just what was wrong and how it was going to get fixed. He said, "After all, we were on vacation. Let someone else work for a change."

He was so happy about showing me where he grew up, where he went to school and many places he went when he was young. He was happy to be home. I asked him why he left home, and he said there were not enough opportunities. "It's just a small community, not many jobs and no advancements. But, it's a great place to visit and get away for peace and quiet."

We spent the next three weeks boating, sight-seeing and working on the mobile home. We would make mad passionate love several times a week and every time I woke up with him beside me I had the same sense of safety and contentment. As each day passed Steve became happier and more relaxed. We must have taken a million pictures, not sure what we will do with all of them, but it was fun.

Many of his old friends were still living there and he had to have everyone meet me, his girlfriend, I felt proud. We were having so much fun and soon the fun would be over. Steve professed it had been the best time he'd had in years and wanted to stay an extra week. I was so thrilled and certainly had no objections! We made the arrangements and stayed one more week. Nevertheless, it flew by and still didn't seem long enough.

The magic of the vacation stayed with us through the flight home and the ride to my house. First thing in the morning I received a text saying he missed me. I knew it would be difficult to live up to my own convictions before the trip, but now it would even be harder. I didn't even want to think that the magic would end just because we were home.

Chapter Twenty-four

The first week after arriving home, Steve and I had dinner together three times and meet for breakfast twice. It was almost like being on vacation. He was holding me close to him and still kissing me in public. My bubble soon burst and all came to an abrupt end. I just stop hearing from him and again began to doubt myself. My convictions flew out the window.

While we both contended that we needed our space, how could it have come to such a sudden halt after spending four weeks together on a daily basis? The roller coaster seemed to take off again, with me not being ready for the ride. The questions of what happened kept flooding my mind. How could he be like this? Where is he? Doesn't he care about me? Why can't he call and be "normal?" More importantly, why don't I move on, since this is clearly hurting me.

Well I still have my work to keep me busy and there is no reason to just sit around waiting. I dig right in and try to stop worrying about it; even if it is eating me away. I go through hurt, disillusionment and end with anger. That feeling of going backwards invaded my mind. What is a relationship supposed to be? I have been in four marriages that were unhealthily that not only cost me pain, shame, but a lot of money. Where does this put us? I think I need to get out of this relationship but I don't feel it.

Since I need to tile my bedroom and always revert back to writing my feelings down, I decided to combine my efforts. I start one tile at a time. On the back of this first I write 'I'm happy when I am with him'. On tile two, 'He doesn't think about others'. Three, 'He more than pays his own way.' Four, 'He makes me feel like I am being used.' This is going to take a long time getting this floor done. Twenty-five, 'He doesn't want to answer to anyone.' Twenty-six, 'I want freedom he gives that to me.' Thirty-one, 'He is seeing other ladies.' Thirty-two, 'He is only making love to me.' Thirty-eight, 'He was open about what he wanted and how he is, from beginning.' Thirty-nine, 'I am trying to change him, not willing to accept what he said in beginning.' Forty, 'He accepts me as I am, not trying to take anything I don't want to give.' Well, it took most of the day to get that floor down and in the end I think I found my answer.

He is who he is, he does care, and I enjoy being with him. Without him knowing it, he's keeping me on the track that I laid for myself; but it is painful and hard to hold on to. I want my freedom, I don't want to get married, and I don't want anyone moving in with me nor me with them. I am still stuck on the idea that I need to be married to have sex. The need for him to say 'I love you' is for my own self-worth; it is time to stop needing that. I am the one building this wall around my life. Making him everything is destructive to me and I must realize that. The wall must be torn down and I must live my life with putting myself first.

That afternoon, I received a call from an older gentleman friend of mine named Jimmy. He invited me to dinner and I was very happy to accept. He is quite smart and a fine conversationalist. He is not looking for anything but friendship. Dinner was good and we enjoyed our time together. It is possible to go out with someone and not be tied to them.

Finally, the next morning Steve calls and wants to spend the day together. Of course, I jump on it; I know that I should act coy with him but why lie. The day was good and the company was as he always is. He came back to my house and saw my tile job and said he loved it. Would he love it if he knew what was hidden underneath? Not being able to control myself, I started questioning him as to why hasn't he called before this? Was he seeing someone else? His answer was, "Yes, I have lots of friends and enjoy spending time with them." I began to feel my heart drop, but something inside stopped it, it is cool. He continued, "I'm not doing anything with any of them, I just need to be with some one that isn't such high maintenance."

"What does that mean?" I was totally lost.

"When I am with you I have think way too much, I have to work to keep up with you. Being with you is a lot of work. But I enjoy every minute of it. You are an amazing woman, you are ninety-nine percent perfect." He smiles and kisses me.

"Wow," was all I could say.

When he got ready to leave, I tell him I really missed having him with me in the mornings. He agrees with me, tells me he is working on that. The next day it is back to work and I was preparing myself for not seeing him for a few days. I think I am going to find a way of handling this.

For the next four weeks, things continued to be the same. I don't see him for a few days then he is there back in my life. We'd spend the day and evening together, then we have breakfast together. He'd text me in between times to keep up with what is going on. Then one day, he tells me he can stay all night if I want him to. I would love that.

We have dinner at home and after dinner while cleaning up, we talk. We get on the subject of people we know and I ask, "Why me, I am not like any of the other women you see?"

His answer is not what I expected nor thought I would hear. "You are an amazing and smart woman. I respect you more than anyone I know."

Surprise overwhelmed me; I just stood there looking at him. I could feel a tingle moving up my body, feeling more happiness than if he had said he loved me. There seemed to be a light turning on in my heart. I think that I had learned to like myself without confirmation from others. I was learning to love myself through the person I was becoming. I respected myself for the things I believed and did but I had no idea that anyone else did. Just this once I allowed hearing what he said and accepted it for what it was. Was this all I really needed? This is such a small thing but it was the biggest and most important thing missing from my new life.

We had a great time that night and the love making was like flying on clouds. After breakfast we parted and went our own ways. For the next few days, when I didn't hear from him, I was at peace. I worked and went out with friends and I didn't sit waiting for a call from him. The realization came that he would call when he was ready, and I was able to accept that.

Chapter Twenty-five

Good to his world, every couple of weeks he was able to spend the night, we would even leave town for a few days at a time. He had changed, he seemed to enjoy my company, and he seemed to relax more when we were together. But, some things hadn't, there were still those times that it would be a day or so that he wouldn't see me again. I had changed though, and it didn't bother me not hearing from him. I was able to finish my bedroom and start on another room. I finished the work on his new office and even started work on another of his houses.

The holidays were quickly approaching and I wondered what this year would bring. Thanksgiving was the first. I knew that I wouldn't see Steve. His roommate's family would be in town and he would be required to be home. My daughter was hot into a relationship of her own and was invited to spend Thanksgiving with his family. I felt happy for her and resigned myself to being alone and that was alright. To my utter surprise, Steve showed up on my doorstep Thanksgiving Day. We spent a few hours together. He said that I was the one thing he was most thankful for, he had to see me. That was so sweet. I was learning to accept the little things he said and did, but not allow them to become more than what they were meant to be.

Our time apart was coming to be less than our time together. He would come over in the evening just to relax with me. We were spending every Saturday together. I knew seeing him so much was not healthy for me, it would become too easy to depend on him being there. I learned to decline his invitations occasionally. There were so many other things to keep me busy and projects to complete. I was able to finish the second room in my house and finished his second house. Luckily, he had plenty of work to keep me busy for him as well.

I still had Christmas on my mind. I had gotten the kids gifts and sent them off; I agreed to spend a day with my daughter and grand-son. Steve was a question, not sure if I should get him a gift or not. I didn't want him to be embarrassed if he didn't get me anything. In the end, decided to buy him something.

In some ways he seemed to be relying on me, not like a lover or even a girlfriend, but like someone whose opinion he respected. One Saturday, we attended a gun show where they even had kittens to adopt. I knew that his roommate's cat was very sick and didn't have long to live, so I suggested that he bring her a kitten. He wasn't sure but got one. Shortly after that, the cat died and the kitten was there to fill the empty space in her heart.

As each day passed a sense of freedom to enjoy life and what each day would bring. The lingering feelings from that moment Steve told me he respected me, was still making me fly. I was wondering if it was real and would last. I didn't want to question it; that would make it seem unreal.

One night it was tested. Steve and I had spent the day together and decided to eat at home. It was my turn to buy the food (we would alternate the cost of home cooking) and we decided on T-bone steaks. Cooking not being high on my skill list, I wasn't sure how to cook the steaks, so I made them well-done, just the way I liked them. Steve was quite unhappy and barked that I'd ruined the meat and it was inedible. His fix was pouring steak sauce, lots of sauce, on it.

"I am sorry, I was wrong in not asking first." I apologized, thinking to myself that he was mad and this would be the end of our relationship. That thought disappeared as quickly as it had entered my mind. I had to learn to accept and adjust and not be frightened. After eating half of his steak, he fed the rest to the dogs. Oh, well. The dogs were happy!

The next fifteen minutes he spent giving me a cooking lesson and I replied that next time we would do it together. He replied; "We will practice it when we are on vacation for two months next year." It was more of a question than a statement. I agreed that would be a good time to learn how to cook a steak. After he left for the night he called me and said he was sorry for getting mad. He said I was more important than a steak. It was a few days before I heard from him again, but this time, I was okay with it.

Christmas was only days away, and I hadn't even put up one decoration; it still didn't fell like it was a holiday. Was this bad, I don't think so I didn't feel sad or depressed. As one gets older and children are grown and out of the house, holidays aren't the bustling times they used to be. It is a time to thank God for his son and to let those around you know that you care.

One day something came up at work and I texted a question to Steve. When he failed to no answer, I called him and still received no answer. The next day he called and wanted to go to breakfast. We talked about his current house I was working on and said I'd tried to get in touch with him for some advice about what I was doing. "You never answered me," I said.

He replied, "I'm an ass; just don't want you to know how often I think about you." He turned bright red and became very quiet. I know he didn't mean to say so much. To curb his embarrassment, I pretended not to hear.

It was December 23rd and I was getting ready to go to work on Steve's house when I got a call from him asking me to come by the office first. When I got to the office he said it was too close to Christmas to be working. He wanted me to be with him while he did all his chores for the day. We spent the day together, and as always I thoroughly enjoyed being with him. When we're traveling together, I learn so much more about him. He has lots of stories to tell and they give me an understanding of who he is and how he thinks. Around 5:00, he went his way and I went home. Pretty soon, he called and said he really didn't want to stay home. He asked if he could come over and bring dinner. Of course, I answered. How perfect.

When he showed up he had some crab legs. Unfortunately, I don't like fish. But, he cooked them and they were actually good. He has inspired me to try many new things I wouldn't ordinarily try. Then he gave me the second best Christmas gift ever; he was going to spend the next two nights with me. He was so tired that I talked him into taking a nap and after an hour of napping he was ready to make it a night I wouldn't forget. I wonder how I could ever forget any night I have spent with him. I do enjoy my nights alone, but it is nice to have your lover wake up with you in the morning.

Knowing that our relationship has become so comfortable and natural for both of us makes it possible to enjoy any time we are together. It has shown me that caring needs to be giving as well as taking. That love and more importantly friendship can only be healthy if both of these are present.

So I didn't know what this Christmas was going to bring; but it turned into the best one I have had since the children were all young. The opening of my gift was amazing; and the gift I gave myself will last the rest of my life; love and respect for myself.

Now how could our time together ever be without some drama? On the 24th we each had a few things to do so he said he would be back at two if that would work out, I said it would. Well two came and went, so did four, I called him. No answer, six came as did ten, at which time I went to bed. I did hear from him at eight A.M. He said he got busy last night, but it was Christmas and he wanted to see me. I was so temped to tell him I was busy but didn't. He showed up about ten, looking haggard. I asked what happened yesterday; I thought he was coming back about two. He told me he ran into an old girlfriend and they went to his house and got very drunk, so drunk that he fell down and hurt his leg. He assured me that they didn't do anything but talked and he sent her home in a cab. I just told him I agreed that he was an ass.

He said, "Yes I was, I know I never told you this but I don't even think about going to bed with anyone but you."

"It's cool, everything is alright." Now I know what that means.

So we did spend Christmas night together and most of the next day. We went back to our normal way of life, and that is enough for me.

Never an End

As the day starts, it ends, and then starts again.

As seasons come and go, just to do it again.

As for every high, there has to be a low.

As teary eyes become dry and clear.

As the young has to become the old.

As pictures and stories keeps one alive forever.

Is as life ends but, is never over.

8-19-1997

Chapter Twenty-six

Well now it is a new year and this is where I am going to end my story. I have taken you on a trip through what I call my life. It has not always been easy to write or even to remember, but it has helped me. I only hope that in some ways it has helped you.

You may never understand just what it was like to be abused by a family member, those that you should be able to trust. Those that should be helping you build a good and healthy life. I hope that this story will help you to understand. Those of you that know what it is like, I hope this will help you to know that you are not alone and that you can overcome it. I hope that whoever reads this will be willing to help any that are in this position.

With all that happened to me during my youth, when I was too young to even put words to what was happening to me; through the time that I was used by my step-brother, I was still able to come through it. My mother who I always thought was there to love and protect me was only able to think of her own needs, no doubt that her childhood wasn't much better than mine. She taught me that I didn't have the right to have needs, just fulfill the needs of others.

All that I had learned growing up was wrong; it was fear and shame. There was no way I would ever be a normal adult, let alone a wife and mother. Somehow, I did the best that I could and knew that my own children were protected from the things I had to face. It was my obligation to change the course of my life and teach my children the things I didn't learn, kindness, love, caring, and trust. I wanted my children to have what I didn't, the ability to believe in themselves and be confident. Whether I helped them in the process or they learned on their own, each of them has that love I finally found.

Through four marriages that all failed, each man being the same man my step-father was; a user with a destructive personality. It wasn't until I step outside of what I had developed in my mind as the right man, did I finally find a man that was good and worthy. I only regret that I didn't love him. I didn't find love until I first learned to love myself. For a person like me, that turned out to be more difficult to accomplish than one can imagine. All the doubt and shame I put on myself had to be completely removed before I could make progress. It took many tries to truly rid myself of my own obstacles. It was only when I could finally come to terms with myself, was I able to find and accept that one last missing piece.

There were several people along my journey that helped and understood, and at times it was only through them that I found the strength to move on. Some knew what was going on because of their own problems in life; while others, being kind and caring in nature, helped me without understanding what they gave. I only hope that I can do as much for another that is in need.

I truly don't know where my life will lead me; but I know that it will be better than my life has ever been. I know that there will be times that I will make the wrong decisions but I have the confidence that I will be able to handle them, make them right and learn even more. I know that it will be hard to always walk on my appointed journey but, I know what I want for myself and know how to find my way back. I don't know if it's a "normal" life, but I believe that is a healthy life.

I know that along the way I made some wrong decisions, these are ones that I hope to help others from making. Believing in oneself is the most important building block; to be who you want to be and do the things that bring you happiness. You are unique in yourself, follow your heart and be true to yourself. As for love, love yourself first. Then you will be able to love freely with another, while not letting anyone control your life.

Any other love that may be mine or come my way will be enjoyed but, it will not control me or my life. I still don't know why there was such an attraction to Steve or why I was able to really give myself to him and enjoy it, but I thank God. Maybe not all questions need an answer. We may not always be lovers but we will always be friends and respect each other.

My life is not over yet, there is much to see and experience. I hope that by writing and telling my story, a part of me will go on long after I am no longer here. The strangest love story is the story of falling in love with me and learning to respect myself.